Justin

Morris Fenris

Justin, Three Brothers Lodge #1

Copyright 2015 Morris Fenris

Changing Culture Publications

Table of Contents

Chapter 1

Late October, Colorado Mountains...

Jessica Andrews clutched the steering wheel so hard, her knuckles turned white. She was currently driving her old Ford Explorer through the passes in the middle of a snowstorm that was quickly becoming a full-on blizzard. It was the end of September and she'd not even thought about checking the weather report to learn the road conditions. The leaves hadn't even finished changing color, or dropping from their summer homes!

"Why did I decide a job in Colorado was a good idea?" she muttered to herself.

She'd left sunny Arizona two days earlier, with nothing but a suitcase of clothing that she now saw was going to be completely inadequate in her new place of residence. And a small cardboard box that held the few possessions that actually meant something to her. She was running away, and while she knew it wasn't the smartest move to make, she just didn't have the strength to stay and fight.

And it was all on account of her good for nothing ex-boyfriend, Jason Walker!

Just thinking his name put a sour taste in her mouth. She'd been dating the handsome football player for just under a year, and she'd convinced herself that her future was with him. "Guess that was my first mistake!" she said aloud.

She'd taken to talking out loud to herself; occasionally she had even been known to answer her own questions. She didn't consider herself crazy, just fed up!

Jessie had been raised by her elderly grandmother in a nice Christian household where attendance at church every time the doors were open was a foregone conclusion. Her mother and father had been called to missionary work in Africa years before, and when her mother had found out she was pregnant, they had put in a request to return stateside on furlough until after their daughter's birth.

Due to tremendous civil unrest and the rise of several Islamic terror groups in the region where they normally ministered, their return to Africa was delayed by eighteen months. At that time, neither of her parents had felt comfortable taking their young toddler to such a dangerous place. Her maternal grandmother had offered her a home while her parents were overseas, and her parents had gratefully accepted. They were only supposed to be gone a year and then they would return stateside once again.

Before leaving on furlough, they had begun working on a school that would allow native South Africans to study and learn how to become missionaries to their own people. It had been the popular protocol for overseas missionaries, and while they normally supervised these schools, her parents would be returning to the States and someone else would be taking over.

Jessie had been too young to realize the sacrifice that had been made by the adults in her life, but as she grew older, she'd come to realize that without her grandmother's sacrifice, she would have most likely died right next to her parents four months after their return to missionary work. Their deaths had been brutal and designed to send terror throughout the land. The Muslims didn't want the Westerner's coming into their land with promises of hope and Christianity. Their murderers had raided the school compound, brutally murdered everyone inside, and then filmed it and placed the films on the internet. The videos had been horrific, and as a result, other American missionaries in the region had been called home.

Jessie had been told all of this when she turned sixteen and started asking questions about her parents. Her grandmother had tearfully showed her the newspaper clippings and magazine articles written in response to the brutal murder of her parents and their entire missionary team. In all, nine Americans had been murdered that day. Thirty-three South Africans had also been killed, amongst them nine children under the age of ten.

That day had been a turning point for Jessie, although she kept her thoughts to herself until she'd graduated the next year and headed off to college. She always considered her parents heroes. They'd abandoned the comforts of home to help bring hope to a desolate land and its people. But after reading the articles, and doing some of her own research, she'd come to the conclusion that only an insane person would have willingly gone back to the region.

She blamed God for not protecting the very people he had sent to such a dangerous place. Her parents had been doing His work, and He'd allowed them to die, leaving her an orphan and hurting. What good was it to follow a God who wouldn't protect you? She'd managed to hide her broken faith from her grandmother as she finished high school, but her anger had only built inside, until she'd finally found an outlet.

Once she'd arrived on the college campus, she'd done her best to partake in all the things she knew went against her Christian upbringing. Parties. Drugs. Alcohol. And then she'd met Thomas in her first classroom clinical. He'd been a bright young man of eighteen, and throughout her sophomore year, she and Thomas became great friends. And then he'd been struck down with an aggressive childhood cancer. He died three months after being diagnosed, and once again, Jessica was left trying to come to terms with a God that allowed a little boy to die in such pain, and his parents to suffer so much grief.

She'd retreated into herself, abandoning the parties and every other social activity at school. She'd been immersed in her grief, and when she met Jason Walker at the end of her junior year, she was merely going through the motions.

Jason drew her out of herself, sweeping her off her feet and bringing a smile to her face for the first time in almost a year. Her teachers all commented on the difference, and even though a little voice inside told her that she was compromising her values to be with him, she became his steady campus girlfriend. She was the eye candy and easygoing girlfriend who demanded nothing and made him look good.

He was a receiver for the football team, a senior, and a promising future as a lawyer awaiting him. He was gorgeous and sought after by lots of girls on campus. But he'd chosen to spend his time with Jessica and that had made her feel special in a way she'd never felt when dating boys before him. She'd managed to retain some of her upbringing, never quite able to abandon her ideas about morality because of her grandmother. Jason had encouraged her to give up the few friends she'd made, telling her they were holding her back and asking too many questions. She'd done so readily, not really needing them, just needing an escape from her reality that Jason constantly provided. He created a fantasy world for her, and she lived there happily.

They'd both graduated and while he'd started law school, she'd begun working on her Master of Education. She'd been convinced that the lack of true emotion she felt for Jason was a good thing and her problem, not his. She'd talked herself into believing that a true emotional connection led only to heartache, and if she could just keep her distance, and still enjoy the benefits of being in a relationship, everything would be fine. The fact that Jason had been willing to keep his emotional distance as well had been seen as a bonus, not a warning sign!

But then she'd received a phone call in March just before completing her master's degree. The call had been the pastor of her grandmother's church, notifying her that her grandmother had passed away. Jessie had gone home a week early for Spring Break, packed up the few things she held dear, and given the rest to charity. The house had been sold and she'd used it to pay off her student loans, and stuck the rest of it in the bank.

Something had shifted in her thinking through that experience. Once again, she blamed God for taking someone she loved, the only family she had left in this world, away from her. She'd returned to school, determined to show Him what she thought about His kind of love. She'd ignored the doubts and inner voice that cautioned her she was going down a slippery slope, and forged ahead. She'd been determined to prove to herself and God that she didn't need His brand of help or guidance in her life.

She'd shoved her inner voice to the side, and even when it had been screaming at her that Jason was playing her, she'd ignored it. She'd convinced herself she was happy, and that Jason's recent inattention was just a phase their relationship was going through. She'd been so wrong!

The car's tires slipped on a patch of ice as she drove across one of the many bridges on this strip of road and she yanked the wheel into the slide, gritting her teeth as she brought the car back under control. *Guess that chapter in the driver's ed book wasn't a waste after all! I certainly would never have put it to good use living in Arizona!*

The car slipped again, this time careening towards the metal guardrail and she gripped the steering wheel so tightly her hands hurt. She took her foot off the gas pedal and looked steadily ahead. She could barely see the white line at the right side of the road now, and the way the snow was falling, she figured that wouldn't last much longer.

"I should have pulled off at the last town!" She'd filled up on gas at a small station and she'd ignored the conversations going on around her about the potential road closure coming. She'd hurried back into her car, pressing hard on the accelerator as she climbed in elevation and headed for the next mountain pass. The snow had been falling steadily for over an hour when she approached the bottom of Vail Pass. Two State Patrol cars had been parked there, the men unlocking the gate that would effectively shut down that stretch of highway until the storm passed. She drove straight through, pretending she didn't see them try to wave her down and stop her. "Dumb, Jess. Really dumb!"

An hour later and the highway was completely snow packed, and large flakes were coming down so fast, she was hard pressed to tell where the road began and ended. The white line was nonexistent, and she only prayed she was actually still driving on pavement and not the shoulder of the highway. She had her headlights on, even though it was still early afternoon, wanting to make sure she could be seen by any other vehicles on the road. *Not that there were any still moving!*

She passed several passenger cars that had pulled off the road, but there didn't seem to be any people in them. She guessed they had hitched a ride with other vehicles that were more suited to the snowy conditions, rather than be trapped on the mountain when night fell.

That thought was terrifying to Jessica so she kept moving forward. She reached the top of a big hill and briefly glimpsed a sign proclaiming it the "summit". It listed the elevation, but the numbers were already obscured by blowing snow that had partially covered the sign.

The highway seemed to be headed downward now, but it had also gotten icier as well. She found herself switching the aging SUV into low gear, thankful she wasn't having to apply her brakes quite as often, but wondering how long they would keep working before they overheated and gave out.

Her vehicle was in serious need of some maintenance, but as a struggling college student, she hadn't had the money in her budget for car repairs. Her grandmother had offered to help out however she could, but Jessica also knew her grandmother lived on a fixed income that was barely enough to keep one human being alive. She'd not wanted to burden her, and so she'd developed a policy of only telling her grandmother what she needed to know. The fact that her car had been in danger of falling into pieces was not on that list! Then her grandmother had died...

She looked at the gauges on her dashboard and bit her bottom lip. "Oh man! That is so not what I need right now." The thermostat was showing on the hot side! She rolled down the windows and turned the heater up to full blast, hoping to pull the extra heat away from the engine so she could keep making her way to the next town.

She'd missed the green sign informing travelers of that distance, and she only hoped it wasn't very far. A little voice inside her urged her to pray for help, but she ignored it. As she had been ignoring it for the last six years. She could do this, if she just kept inching forward. She would do this!

She might have made it too, if she'd kept her eyes glued to the road. But while she'd been fiddling with the heater, she'd failed to notice the large white truck parked off the road. She also hadn't been aware that she was driving more off to the side of the road than in her lane.

When she slammed into the back of the vehicle, both facts were made known to her as she hit the steering wheel with her forehead. She felt her car come to an abrupt stop; the sound of metal hitting metal ringing in her ears just before everything went black.

Chapter 2

Three Brothers Lodge, just above Silver Springs, Colorado…

Justin Donnelly lifted the pan of lasagna from the oven and sat it on the stove. "Grub's ready," he called out to the two men he felt privileged to call brothers. They all worked together in the outfitting and guide business they'd inherited from their uncle. They also volunteered as firemen in the small town at the base of the mountain where they lived, and they were the key personnel in the search and rescue team for the county.

It was a perfect combination of being outdoors, helping people, and not having to wear a suit and tie to work every day. The three brothers couldn't imagine living anywhere else or doing anything else.

As winter had come suddenly to Colorado, their lives became much less complex and all three of them were looking forward to the holidays and a slower pace around the lodge where they lived. They'd just completed one of their best tourist seasons ever, and with the exception of a few backcountry hunting trips still scheduled, they were ready to settle in for the winter and relax.

Mason and Kaillar wandered towards the kitchen table, sniffing as they took their seats. "Smells good, man."

"Thanks. I made enough for leftovers as well," Justin told them, pulling out his chair and having a seat. They always made twice as much food as they would eat in one sitting, having gotten into the habit of eating leftovers the next day; it took the burden off of everyone in the household.

The men all took turns cooking and doing the laundry, and tonight was Justin's turn. He'd made his signature dish: lasagna, garlic bread and a tossed salad. Mason and Kaillar had just returned from a three-day hiking trip and he knew the pasta dish would be welcome. "So, how did things look up there?" he asked, scooping a generous portion of the lasagna onto his plate.

"Quite a bit of bear activity still, considering how much snow's already fallen," Mason said. He was the youngest Donnelly brother, having just turned 22 a few weeks back. He was the only one to have taken any college classes, but he'd quit over a year ago, the classroom having no more appeal for him. He wanted to be out in nature, not sitting in a classroom learning about it from a book!

"There's another storm brewing out there right now. I wouldn't be surprised if we didn't get a few feet out of this one," Kaillar added. He knew the ski slopes would be rejoicing at so much new snow, and he was right there with them. He loved to ski and was looking forward to his fifth year on the ski patrol team. He'd also started a youth ski-racing program several years earlier, and was looking forward to the competition season starting up again. He had some very promising youngsters on his team, and was looking forward to seeing them reach their full potential.

"I hope everyone out there pays attention to the weather reports. It would be nice to get through this month without any major incidents." Justin's hope was echoed by his brothers. It seemed every year about this time, at least one hiker, group of college kids, or motorist decided to test their mettle against the mountains. Funny thing – the mountains almost always won! Especially with winter arriving so suddenly. The mountains were unpredictable right now, and getting caught unaware in one of the first major snowstorms of the season was never a good idea.

"This storm's going to blow over fairly quick. Couple of days at most."

"Good thing. We have hunters coming in next week. Any idea where we're going to take them?" Kaillar asked, referring to the upcoming big game rifle season that was set to begin in just a few short days.

"Yeah. I think so. I didn't have a chance to collect the game cameras this afternoon." Justin glanced at the clock hanging on the wall above the stove and nodded his head. "Maybe I should run up and collect them before it gets any worse out there." He took a look out the large picture windows in the front of the lodge and then changed his mind. "On second thought, maybe not. It's really starting to come down."

"We can go get them when the storm's over. The hunters aren't due in until Sunday night," Mason reminded him.

"Good." Justin sat back down and dug into his own meal.

The three brothers knew the mountains around their lodge like the back of their hands. They'd been guiding hunters for the last five years now, and found the additional income came in handy during the long months of winter. They occasionally hunted themselves, having first learned with their uncle when they were too young to get their own licenses.

They had thrived under their uncle's guidance, something that never happened while in their mother's care. Their mother, Maria Donnelly, had left Silver Springs more than thirty years earlier. The small mountain town of two hundred people was not nearly exciting enough for her. Her quest for fame and fortune had taken her first to Los Angeles, and eventually on to Las Vegas.

Unfortunately, her talents hadn't been spectacular enough to earn her a place among the stars of the movie screen and she'd quickly wound up getting involved with the wrong crowd. Drugs and alcohol had taken over her life, and then she'd gotten pregnant with Justin.

She'd come back to Colorado, but the strain of trying to live up to her parents' expectations had sent her fleeing back to Las

Vegas, back to the boyfriend who'd discovered she was willing to do almost anything to score her next bag of heroin.

Her brother, Jed, had gone to Las Vegas and hauled her back several times, but nothing had been able to break her addiction to the drugs. She'd tried two more times to get her life together, coming home before Mason was born, and then again after Kaillar had entered the world, but the lure of the drugs always won over her responsibility to the three little boys she'd brought into the world.

When Justin was four, she'd run for the last time – leaving her three children behind with her brother. The Las Vegas authorities had called a few days later to say they had found her body badly beaten and abandoned in one of the seedier parts of the city.

Jed had gone down and collected her body; returning home, he'd arranged for her to be buried next to her parents. Her father had died of a heart attack shortly after Justin had been born, and her mother died of a broken heart a short time later. With no other siblings, her children had been parentless, but not without family.

Jed had applied to become their permanent guardian, and the once confirmed bachelor had become an instant father of three little boys, ages four, two and six months. His sister had neither known nor cared who the fathers of her children were. Jed had more than made up for their absence. He'd treated the three boys as his own, but rather than allowing them to call him dad, he'd made sure they kept the familial connection straight by calling him Uncle Jed.

He'd made many sacrifices for the three boys, leaving behind his preference for a solitary life on his mountain to that of regular interaction with the small town below. He'd learned to socialize with the townsfolk for his nephews' sake. Something the three brothers would never forget.

He'd passed away several years earlier. Justin had been working overseas as a helicopter pilot in the Middle East, making tons of money by putting himself into dangerous situations. When he'd received the call about his beloved Uncle Jed, he'd quit and come home. And he was still here several years later.

Mason and Kaillar had both expressed a desire to take their Uncle Jed's outfitting operation to the next level. With their uncle's life insurance money, and Justin's more than adequate savings account, they'd remodeled the lodge where they'd grown up, built several tourist cabins, and become well known as one of the best guide services in this part of Colorado.

The phone rang and Kaillar got up to answer it. A few minutes later, he replaced the receiver and frowned at his brothers. "We might have a situation."

"Might have?" Justin inquired, never having met a situation that was stuck in limbo. Either it was a situation requiring their assistance, or it wasn't. "What's up?"

"That was Shelby over at the Frisco dispatch office. She said a vehicle got through the snow gates at the west side of Vail just as the patrolmen were closing the gates. They tried to wave the driver back, but the vehicle just kept going."

"Oh, yeah?" Mason asked. "They're on the pass?"

"Shelby assumes so. That was over an hour ago and they've been monitoring the cameras along the highway for the vehicle. An older model Ford Explorer, dark blue with a rack on top. Arizona license plates."

"Maybe they missed it?" Mason offered.

Kaillar shook his head. "Shelby doesn't think so. They have the vehicle passing the summit thirty minutes ago, but it never made it to the next camera."

Justin was silent, and then he confirmed what they were all thinking. "Well, that only leaves about two miles of highway. Maybe they pulled off…"

"They never made it to the Minturn turn-off."

Justin looked at his brothers and then made a decision. "I'll take a tracker out and look for the vehicle. You two just got back and need some down time."

"Not happening. You know the cardinal rule is that we never go on a search and rescue op without backup. Since we're the only available backup, which means you're stuck with us tagging along."

"Any other vehicles up there that haven't shown up?" Justin asked, starting to put the leftover food away in the fridge. If they were going out in the weather, he wanted to make sure everyone that might be stranded was located.

"Shelby mentioned something about two other vehicles as well. There's something else you should probably know."

"Yeah?" Justin asked. The more information, the more efficient he could be. The fact that the missing vehicle had Arizona plates meant the driver might have no experience whatsoever in winter driving conditions. A sure recipe for disaster in a storm like the one currently raging outside.

"The vehicle's being driven by a woman. They have her on camera at the Edwards pullout getting gas. The attendant remembered her because she looked completely exhausted."

"And they're sure they saw her car pass the summit?" Justin asked, already thinking how nasty checking the pass was going to be tonight. Even just two miles of it.

"Yeah. Her car headed down thirty minutes ago." Kaillar looked at his brothers and then stated, "They're asking for our help to find everyone and get them to safety. At this point, the weather forecast is looking much worse than they originally thought. It's going to get cold tonight when the snow stops. Really cold. They're saying it could hit the low teens."

Justin shoved the leftover lasagna into the fridge and then headed out of the kitchen. "Well, then I guess we better get geared up and head out before it gets dark. We've only got a few hours of daylight left, and I don't want to be checking those roads in the dark."

"Me either. I'll go get the trackers out." Mason took two more bites of his dinner and then headed for the front doors of the lodge. "Might start a new pot of coffee to take with us as well."

Kaillar was already in the kitchen, his mind on the same wavelength as his brother's. "I'll meet you all in the barn."

Justin nodded and then headed for the stairs that led to the bedroom suites the brothers each occupied. He pulled his cell phone from his pocket as he climbed the stairs, placing a call to Jeremy Phillips, the pastor of the small church in Silver Springs.

"Justin?" Jeremy answered, concern evident in his voice.

"Hi, Pastor. Sorry to disturb your afternoon."

"No problem. What's up?"

Justin sighed. "We're heading out in a few minutes to check the pass. Shelby called from Frisco and they've got several vehicles on the pass that haven't reached the other side yet. We're going to try and find them before dark."

"Son, you and your brothers have my prayers. What can I do to help?"

"That's more than enough. I just wanted to let you know that I might not make practice tomorrow morning."

"Justin, don't worry about that. I'll get one of the high school boys to step in and help with basketball practice. If we even have it. This storm's looking rather fierce at the moment."

"Thanks, Pastor. Gotta go."

"May heavenly angels guide your steps this afternoon."

Amen! Justin pocketed his phone and grabbed his winter gear from the closet. His uncle had made sure his nephews went to church and had the opportunity to develop their own relationship with God while they were growing up. Each of them had taken their own path to get there, but Justin had no doubts in his mind that the Donnelly brothers were God-fearing, Christian men. He'd seen firsthand the power of prayer, and he never missed an opportunity to allow the good people of Silver Springs to put their faith into action.

He headed to the barn, seeing that his brothers were already out there and almost ready to go. Joining hands, he met their eyes, and in a tradition that had been first started by their uncle, they bowed their heads and asked for divine guidance for the next few hours.

"Amen. Mount up, boys." Justin climbed aboard his tracker, the large enclosed vehicle that was the perfect fit for snowy mountain roads. There were skis on the front, and large snow tracks on the rear. The vehicles could only go about thirty miles an hour, but that didn't worry Justin. According to Shelby, they only needed to check about two miles of highway. Under normal conditions, that would take less than an hour, but in this storm, two miles were going to feel like twenty!

Chapter 3

A half hour later, the Donnelly boys arrived at the highway and they split up. Justin and Kaillar took the eastbound lanes, with Mason taking the westbound lanes. Shelby had called back just as they were reaching the highway stating that two people had just walked in, having gotten a ride from another motorist into Frisco. The problem was of a medical nature, the man desperately needing the medication he'd forgotten in their car. They had pulled over just beyond the turnoff that led to Silver Springs.

Mason had offered to go down, retrieve the pills, and drive them into Frisco. From there, he'd spend the night with friends if it got too late, or he'd take the ridge trail home. Justin and Kaillar would locate the missing vehicles, three of them according to information they'd been given.

Within the first mile, Justin and Kaillar came across the first two vehicles. They had pulled off the highway within thirty yards of each other, making recovery of the people quick and easy. A single businessman occupied the first car, and two college boys occupied the second. All three were grateful for the rescue and Kaillar loaded them into his tracker and headed back to the highway turnoff. There was a small motel in Silver Springs, run by a native of Silver Springs and widower, Sarah Jenkins. She would be more than willing to put up the stranded travelers for a night or two.

Justin continued up the eastbound lane. He was almost at the two miles that would put him at the next camera location when he saw the bright yellow of headlights covered in snow off to the side. As he approached the vehicle, he realized there was a second vehicle, a white oversized truck parked in front of it. It wasn't until he was right up on the cars that he realized the SUV had crashed into the truck.

He quickly parked his tracker and checked the truck first. It was empty and had an orange patrol tag on the windshield indicating the vehicle had been abandoned there prior to the start of the storm.

The small SUV was a different story. It matched the description of the vehicle that had slipped through the gates just before they were closed. A woman was crumpled against the steering wheel. He tried the door, but it was locked. He rapped his knuckles on the window, but she was completely unresponsive.

A gust of wind and a new shower of snow sent him back to the tracker for something to break the window with. He used the handle of his safety axe to smash the rear passenger window. Once he had the glass cleared, he reached inside and unlocked the doors with the electric locks. He wasn't sure how long it had been since the crash, but the battery was still working and for that, he was thankful.

He hurried around to the driver's side door and eased it open. His brows lifted at the attire of the occupant. She had on a pair of thin pants made of a stretchy material, with only a thin t-shirt covering her upper torso. He glimpsed a lightweight jacket sitting on the seat next to her purse and her cell phone sitting in a holder on the dashboard.

"Ma'am? Can you hear me?" he asked her, removing his glove and placing his warm fingers along the side of her neck. Her pulse was strong, but she was out cold. And her skin was icy to the touch. There was a small trickle of blood running down past her ear, and he gently lifted the blonde locks up, seeing a large bruise on her forehead. A small cut near the edge of the bruise was the source of the blood. He reached for the box of tissues sitting in the passenger seat and dabbed at it. He reached for her purse, grabbed her wallet and discovered that her name was Jessica Andrews.

"Jessica? Can you hear me? I need you to open your eyes and tell me if you're hurt anywhere besides your head. Come on now, sugar. Open your eyes." Justin jiggled her shoulder slightly, not wanting to cause her further injury by moving her without first clearing her neck and spine. Normally, he'd wait for backup to get there and then remove her, being careful to keep her spine straight. He'd place a collar around her neck as well – everything possible to prevent aggravating any hidden spinal cord injury that might be present. He'd seen firsthand what could happen when those extra protocols weren't followed, but extreme situations called for extreme measures.

He didn't have that luxury of following all the safety protocols right now. The snow was continuing to fall, the sun was preparing to set, and it was mighty cold outside! And only going to get colder! He shivered and called to her again, placing his icy hand against her cheek. "Jessica! Open your eyes! Now!" He raised his voice, hoping to get some response from her.

She moaned and slowly her eyelids started to flutter. She opened them a few seconds later and Justin felt his heart jump inside his chest. Her eyes were the most unusual color of green he'd ever seen. He lowered his voice: "Welcome back. My name is Justin and I'd love to get you out of the cold and someplace warm, but I need to know if you're hurt anywhere besides that nasty bump on your head."

She blinked slowly and then groaned as she pushed herself back in the seat. She lifted a small hand to her forehead and then winced when she touched the large bruise forming there. "What happened?"

"Well, my guess is that you ran into the back of that truck," Justin nodded towards the large truck sitting a few feet away.

She started to nod and then winced. "Yeah. I remember it came out of nowhere. Is anyone hurt?"

"There wasn't anyone in the truck. It was abandoned before the storm started. You ran into it."

"Why didn't they pull it off the road!" she asked, her voice rising slightly. Hysteria was close to the surface and she tried to keep it at bay.

"They did. You weren't driving on the road."

Her shoulders slumped as she realized she could have just as easily ran her vehicle off the side of a cliff. She closed her eyes. "That explains it. I couldn't see…" She opened her eyes and looked outside where night was falling fast. "It's still snowing."

"It sure is and we need to get off this mountain pretty quick. Do you think you can walk if you lean on me?"

"Where would we go?" she asked, closing her eyes again in obvious distress.

"Well, as much as I'd like to get you down to the hospital tonight, I don't think that's wise now that it's getting dark. My brothers and I run a lodge about five miles from the summit. It will be warm and dry there until morning."

Jessica opened her eyes and glanced at him. "My head hurts."

"We'll get you something for that as well. Now, hand me your purse and I'll go put it into the tracker and then come back for you. Is there anything else you need out of your vehicle tonight?"

"I only have one suitcase and a cardboard box with me."

"Okay. Do you need them tonight?" he inquired, wanting to get moving soon.

"Maybe the suitcase?" she asked softly.

"Got it. Sit tight and I'll come help you in just a few minutes." Justin retrieved her suitcase and then put it and her purse in the back seating area of the tracker. The snow was making things very slippery. He grabbed her keys and then held onto her arm as she slowly swung her legs out of the car.

When she slipped on the road, he looked down and realized she was wearing tennis shoes. Her short stature was hard to miss and he placed her at 5'6" and maybe one hundred and ten pounds. She was much too thin to his way of thinking, and he found himself wanting to feed her one of his home-cooked meals.

He felt her shiver and realized he'd allowed his mind to wander. Smiling through the falling snow, he placed a guiding arm around her shoulders, urging her towards the tracker and their salvation.

The snow was already above her ankles, and he smiled when she said with a grimace, "I already hate snow!"

"Best get used to it if you plan on staying in Colorado long. Winter's not even officially here yet."

"Great!" she told him, once again regretting her decision to move here. She'd wanted a change of scenery and to get away from Arizona. "You've certainly accomplished that! What were you thinking, Jess?"

Justin looked down at her. "Excuse me?"

Jessica blushed, realizing she'd just spoken her thoughts out loud. She would definitely have to work on that bad habit. Otherwise, the people she'd yet to meet would definitely think she was missing a few screws in her head.

"Sorry. I was talking to myself."

"Ah. Well, don't worry about it. I've been known to do that a time or two myself." They reached the tracker and he opened the door, helping her get situated on the vinyl seat and then pulling the safety strap across her lap and fastening it.

"Thank you," she murmured to him just before he could shut the door. Her head hurt, but not so much that she didn't get a whiff of his aftershave. It was one of her favorites and one she'd always wanted Jason to wear, but he'd been adamant that he didn't like the way it smelled on him. *In reality, it was his fiancée who hadn't liked the way her favorite cologne smelled.* "I was such an idiot!"

He looked into her eyes and smiled. "Well, I don't know that I would agree with that. And you are very welcome. Let's get you back to the lodge and warmed up." He'd noticed she was shivering, so he slipped his jacket off and draped it across her front.

"Wait! I can't…"

"You're freezing. I'll be fine, and the tracker has a really good heater. Sit tight." Justin quickly made his way around to the driver side and climbed in. He cranked the heater up on high and slowly turned the tracker around, heading it back down the mountain.

He grabbed the radio and called Kaillar first. "Kai, you there?"

"I'm here. I just finished getting the travelers set up in Silver Springs. Did you find the other vehicle?"

"Yeah. I've got her. She's got a nasty bump on her head, but I don't want to try taking her all the way to Frisco in the dark."

"Roger that. It's really getting nasty out there. I'm looking at the Doppler radar for the mountain and this storm isn't going away anytime soon."

"Got it. Have you heard from Mason?"

"Yeah, he's good as well. Got the man his meds and he's going to head over to Jenna's for the night. She and Tyler are in Denver so their place is empty. He'll head home once the storm clears."

"That sounds good. I'm heading home with Jessica. With that bump on her head, I don't want to leave her alone tonight. You heading back up to the lodge?"

"Yeah, in a bit."

"Good. Do me a favor – stop by the clinic and see if Dr. Matthews is working this afternoon. If he is, tell him to expect a call from me in an hour."

"Will do. She going to be okay tonight?"

Justin glanced at his passenger. Her face was pale, her eyes closed with a frown between her eyes. She was in pain, but before he could do anything about that, he wanted to make sure she didn't have a concussion or any other injuries that might require immediate medical intervention.

"Justin?"

"Yeah, I'm here. I think she's gonna be fine. I'll know once I get her back to the lodge."

"Okay. I'll find the doc for you. Be careful getting home."

"I will. See you in a bit."

Chapter 4

Jessica huddled under the jacket of the man sitting next to her. Her head was throbbing in time with her heartbeat, her feet had begun to thaw out and were soaking wet, and she realized she was now headed to some isolated cabin with a man she didn't know.

But he rescued you, so doesn't he get some points for that? I mean, how many guys would come out in the middle of a blizzard to rescue people who didn't have the common sense to know they should have pulled off at the last town?

Jessica closed her eyes and wished the seat was tall enough to lean her head back on. It was growing darker by the minute, the storm having completely obliterated the waning sun. She turned her attention to the man next to her, his hands expertly steering the machine across the expanse of snow with the confidence of someone who'd done the same thing many times before.

They'd left the highway five minutes earlier, and were now making their way through the forest. She didn't see any signs to guide their way, and she only hoped he truly did know where he was going.

She tried to see where they were going, but the headlights only lit up a small area of the ground in front of them and lots of very tall trees. A sense of claustrophobia assailed her and she swallowed to try and stem a growing sense of fear.

"You hanging in there?" Justin asked, his baritone voice soft in the relative silence of the late afternoon.

"Umm…We're not lost, are we?" she asked before she could stop herself.

Justin chuckled. "No. We're not lost. In fact," he reached across her and pointed to her right. "If you keep your eyes fixed over there you should see the lights of the lodge in just…about…*now*." He slowed the tracker down as they rounded the last stand of trees and watched her face as she caught sight of the lodge for the first time.

It was a two-story log cabin, very large with a wraparound porch and rustic log furniture situated here and there. Everything was covered with a fine dusting of snow, and she looked at it with a look of wonder upon her face. "It's like something from a Christmas card."

To the right of the lodge stood a very rustic, and yet modern-looking barn. Corral fences, partially buried in the snow drifts, stretched out from either side, and the red metal roof was only visible in small patches where the snow had yet to pile up.

Justin chuckled. "Well, I don't know about that. Let's get the tracker put away and then I'll show you where you can clean up a bit. I want to check your head out as well and I'm trusting you to let me know if you have any other aches or pains."

Jessica nodded, never taking her eyes from the log cabin. There was something about it that was so comfortable and welcoming; she felt tears sting her eyes. It looked like a home! She hadn't felt that way since the last time she'd been home while her grandmother was still alive. Remembering that visit brought more tears to her eyes. *I was so horrible and secretive.*

Her grandmother had known something wasn't right, but even though she'd asked, Jessica hadn't been able to tell her grandmother how far from her values she'd fallen. Her grandmother would have been so disappointed in her. *But not as disappointed as I am in myself.*

Her grandmother had tried to get her to go and speak with the pastor of the small church she'd grown up in, and Jessica still remembered how hurt her grandmother had been as Jessica proceeded to tell her that she didn't need a pastor to diagnose what was wrong with her. And she certainly didn't need God to fight her battles for her.

In her mind, God was the reason for her troubles. He'd taken her parents, never allowing her to have a healthy relationship with the two adults who should have been a major influence in her life. And then she'd allowed her blind faith to translate from a spiritual one into a romantic one. And it had let her down. She couldn't trust herself, and she definitely didn't feel like she could trust the God who'd let her parents die. She wasn't sure she had any trust left in her when it came to her emotions.

She lost the battle to stem her tears. When they spilled over, she reached up and wiped them away, unaware that her companion had seen her.

"Hey! Why the tears?" Justin asked, concern in his voice.

Jessica shook her head and then immediately regretted the movement. "Ow! Sorry, I'm just tired." She didn't want to analyze the reason for her tears, and she definitely didn't want a stranger passing judgment on her.

Justin looked at her and she held his gaze until he nodded and looked away. He started the tracker moving forward again and drove it straight into the barn. Once he had the barn doors secured, he helped her down and then grabbed her purse and her suitcase. When he slipped the strap of her purse over his shoulder, she couldn't contain her grin.

"What?" he asked her.

Jessica bit her lip and then told him, "You put my purse over your shoulder like a pro. Do you carry your wife's purse a lot?"

Justin glanced at her purse and then laughed at himself. "No wife."

"Girlfriend, then."

Justin shook his head, escorting her out the side door and down the covered walkway. "No girlfriend. And to my knowledge this is the first purse I've ever worn on my shoulder."

"Really?" she asked as if she didn't quite believe him. *This gorgeous guy doesn't have a girlfriend or a wife? What's wrong with him?* She'd been observing him since he rescued her and right off the top of her head, she couldn't answer her own question. He seemed like a genuinely nice, straightforward guy. A rarity for sure.

"Really." He took her elbow as they climbed the four steps leading up to the porch. "Watch your step." He opened the door and then allowed her to enter first.

Jessica couldn't see enough as she stepped inside his home. An open concept allowed her to see through most of the lower level, her view only obstructed by the large staircase that led upstairs. A large fireplace took up the wall to her left, bracketed on both sides by floor-to-ceiling windows. Comfortable couches and chairs were arranged in front of the hearth, with colorful throw pillows and blankets draped here and there. The place was huge!

Polished wood floors gleamed throughout and vibrant area rugs tied everything together just so. The lighting fixtures were even a bit rustic, with a huge antler chandelier hanging over the foyer.

"This place is amazing!"

Justin looked around his home and then shrugged. "We call it home."

Jessica continued to turn her head, trying to take in everything and failing. To her right, a large pool table with dark wood and red felt occupied the space. Behind it, a wooden bar stood with stools in front and a gleaming, polished wood bar top, and a large mirrored wall behind. She sniffed the air and realized there was a wonderful smell of basil and garlic in the air.

Justin was watching her and then he smiled. "Hungry?"

Jessica bit her lip again and nodded. "I could eat."

"Good. Come on back to the kitchen with me. I made lasagna earlier this morning and we had just finished eating when we got the call to go rescue some motorists."

"Meaning me?" she asked, feeling guilty for having been the reason this man and his brothers had been out in such nasty weather.

"You were one of the reasons. But you weren't the only one. Kaillar took three people down to Silver Springs a short time before I found you. Speaking of which, come sit down and let me look at your head."

Jessica hung back. "Do you think I could clean up a bit first?"

"Sure. The second door to your right is a bathroom. There should be towels under the sink. Come back out when you're finished and I'll have some dinner heated up for you." He watched her walk away, finding himself curious about her story. She'd been travelling very light, and yet she wasn't dressed for a Colorado winter. Her driver's license had been from Arizona, and he wondered if she was just passing through.

He retrieved the lasagna from the fridge and placed a healthy portion on two plates. While they reheated in the microwave, he placed a call to Doc.

"So, how's your traveler?" Doc asked without preamble.

"Well, she's got a goose egg on her forehead with a small cut, but it had already stopped bleeding by the time I got to her. She seems to be ambulating okay and no dizziness to speak of."

"How are her pupils and color?"

"She's got good color in her cheeks and her pupils seem to be reacting normally."

"Well, she sounds fine so far. Headache?"

"Yeah, she did complain of a little headache, and my guess is she's going to have some muscle soreness by tomorrow."

"She could take a couple of over-the-counter painkillers tonight for the headache. I don't want to give her anything too strong. A good night's sleep will go a long way toward recovery."

"She looks pretty tuckered out. I figure she's been driving nonstop for the last few days. There's dark circles under her eyes and she looks a little thin to me."

Doc cleared his throat and then asked, "Do I sense more than a passing interest in your guest?"

Justin chuckled. "Trying to fix me up?"

"Sounds like you're well on the way to fixing yourself up. Can't say it would hurt my feelings to see you boys happily married and settled down."

"We'll get around to it one of these days. Don't worry."

"Oh, I'm not worried. But you're the last three bachelors in Silver Springs, and with everyone else married and already having babies, you and them brothers of yours are lagging behind."

Justin laughed. "Not every single male in Silver Springs is married."

"No, the ones that aren't are either too old to be thinking of such things, or still in need of their mommas taking care of them. All I'm saying is when a single young woman comes to town, whether by accident or not, you shouldn't pass up an opportunity to test the waters."

"Thanks for the advice," Justin told him, not taking offense since it seemed most of the older folk in town had decided the Donnelly brothers were in need of help finding their wives. The ladies' circle at church had even tossed around the idea of inviting the single adults from the neighboring towns to a Friday night get-together.

So far, Pastor Jeremy had been successful in staving them off, but with the holidays fast approaching, he'd heard the rumblings again and it seemed matchmaking was in the air. Justin made a mental note to pass the warning along to his brothers.

He heard the faucet in the bathroom turn off and opened the microwave door. He removed the plates of lasagna and then set them on the table. He added slices of crusty bread and two glasses of ice water. He was just placing the butter on the table when she reappeared in the doorway. He glanced up and asked, "Feel better?"

Jessica nodded slowly and then walked forward. "It smells delicious."

"Thanks. How's the head?"

"It's okay. Sore. Maybe I could have some ice?"

Justin shook his head, opening the freezer drawer and pulling out a frozen bag of peas, "Better than ice. It conforms to your body part."

Jessica took the bag of peas and the dishtowel he handed her, placing it on her forehead before commenting, "You speak as if from experience."

"I have two brothers, and more experience than I like to remember."

"You and your brothers fought a lot?"

"No! But like all boys, we got into lots of mischief. What about you? Any brothers or sisters?"

Chapter 5

Justin didn't expect his question to have such an effect on her. She paled and then turned away from him, returning to the dining table and sitting down. Following her, he asked, "Jessica?"

"Jess."

"What?" he queried, sitting down and watching her carefully.

"My friends call me Jess. Or Jessie."

"Okay. Jess, you never answered my question."

She sighed. "No siblings. Not even any parents I actually remember." *I would have loved to have brothers and sisters.* Growing up, she'd longed for the companionship of someone other than her grandmother. Never one to make friends easily, she'd known a few girls she called friends, but they'd never been the type of friends one hung out with at the mall, or even had sleepovers with. Those types of friends hadn't existed for Jessica while growing up.

"Wow! I'm sorry. About your parents," Justin clarified.

Jess cringed, wishing she could have held back that last statement. *Way to put how you really feel right out there, Jess!*

"Yeah, well they made a decision and it cost them their lives. At least they left me with my grandmother before they allowed themselves to get killed."

Allowed themselves to get killed? Justin reached for the butter. "Your grandmother raised you?" He steered away from the topic of her parents for the moment.

"Yes." Jessica had a smile upon her face, but it was strained.

"What's she think about you moving to the mountains of Colorado?" he asked with an easy smile on his face.

Jessica felt her heart clench, and she mumbled, "She's dead, so it doesn't matter what she thinks."

"Again, I'm sorry." Sensing that a change of subject was needed, Justin picked up his fork and then gestured towards her plate. "Eat, and then maybe we can watch a movie. It's still early."

Jessica set the bag of peas down on the table and placed her napkin in her lap. She took a bite of her food and then looked up at him in surprise, "This is really good."

"Thanks. I enjoy cooking. That was probably what I missed the most when I was over in the Middle East."

"You were in the service?" she asked in shock. He hadn't seemed like the military type. She'd met plenty of air jockeys in Arizona. It was close enough to the airbases in Nevada, and with the pleasant weather and lack of mountains, it made a great place to hold practice drills.

"No. I joined the Civil Air Patrol during high school and learned how to fly fixed-wing planes. When I graduated, I learned how to fly helicopters as well. I took all of the EMT and paramedic courses. One of my instructors took a job over in Saudi Arabia flying medical transports. When he offered to get me a job working over there as well, I jumped at it."

"How old were you?" she asked, taking another bite of her food.

Justin was pleased to see a little color coming back into her cheeks. "Twenty-one. I flew helicopters over there for just under five years. The pay was amazing, more than I could hope to make here in the States in a decade."

34

"What made you come home?" she asked, pushing her plate away when she was finished.

"My uncle died. Like you, we were not raised by our mother."

"What happened?" she asked.

Justin shook his head. "That's a story for another time." He stood and picked up the dirty dishes and carried them back into the kitchen. He rinsed them and then placed them with the dishes from earlier into the dishwasher. He added some soap and turned it on.

Jessica was still sitting at the table when he returned. "Feel like watching a movie?"

She lifted her head and slowly nodded. "Sure. Could I get some pain medicine first though?"

Justin nodded, "Sure." He disappeared and then came back with a small bottle in his hands. He handed it to her and then waited while she took two of the tablets. She pushed her chair back, following him back to the large couches. She settled herself into the corner of one and audibly groaned. She was beginning to feel the effects of the day and could feel her muscles cramping up in response.

"So, what kind of movies do you like to watch?" Justin asked, surveying the large collection he and his brothers had amassed over the years.

"No horror. Maybe a comedy?" she suggested. That was always a safe choice.

"Comedy it is." Justin picked out one of his favorites, a story about a family that took a road trip across the country and the various tragedies that eventually drew them closer together.

"So, you're from Arizona?"

She nodded her head slowly as the movie loaded. "Yeah. I'm starting to think I should have stayed there. Or at least found a job someplace without snow."

"Never been here in the winter?"

She laughed softly. "I've never been out of Arizona until this trip. I guess I thought it didn't snow around here until much later in the year."

"The mountains can get snow as early as Labor Day."

Labor Day? But that was in September. What was I thinking? "Yeah, the Arizona desert is looking better all the time."

"You'll love the Colorado winters if you give them a chance."

"Maybe." She watched as the movie began and several minutes later, she asked him, "Are your brothers coming back tonight?"

"Kaillar is. Mason will spend the night in Frisco and then head home tomorrow or whenever the storm abates."

"I feel horrible that you all had to come out in that nasty storm to find us."

"Don't be. We're all part of the search and rescue team for the county. Finding people who are lost or in need of assistance is what we do."

"Well, thank you. I don't know if I'm ever going to get warm again."

Justin glanced at her T-shirt and then spied her wet socks. She'd removed her tennis shoes, but her socks were wet through. "Why don't you go put on some warmer clothes?"

Jess blushed. "I would if I had any. I figured I would have plenty of time to do some shopping once I got here."

Here? Justin was confused and asked, "Where are you headed?"

Jess looked at him and then smiled. "Here. Silver Springs. I took the job as the new elementary teacher."

Chapter 6

A few hours later, Jess asked if there was some place she could lie down and get some sleep. The stress of the day had caught up with her and she'd been yawning nonstop for the last twenty minutes of the movie. And now that she was warm again, she was having trouble keeping her eyes open.

Justin had slipped upstairs, returning with a red flannel shirt and a pair of dark grey sweatpants that were nice and soft from having been washed so many times. "I realize those are going to be way too big, but they'll be warmer than what you have on right now." He added a pair of white tube socks to the pile of clothing and then suggested she go change before they watched the movie.

She'd done so, rolling the sleeves up on the shirt, and rolling the waistband of the sweatpants down and the ankles up. She knew she probably looked silly, but with the added dryness of the too-large socks, she was warm. That's all that mattered.

"Sure, follow me. We only have two guest rooms in the main lodge."

"Main lodge?" Jess asked, following him as he carried her suitcase around the staircase and to a small hallway on the other side of the house.

"Yeah, we have six guest cabins as well. Each one is slightly different from the others." He stopped in front of a wood door. "So, you're a teacher. How old are you?"

Jess laughed. "Not as young as you think I am. I turned twenty-four last month."

"Twenty-four? Huh."

"How old are you?" Jess asked, thinking that turnabout was fair play.

"Twenty-seven. I'll be twenty-eight at the end of the month."

"Gosh, that old?" Jess teased him. It felt good to laugh, even though there'd been precious little in her life the last six months to evoke such emotion.

"Here it is, and I should probably warn you I'm known for getting even." Justin winked at her as he pushed the door open to reveal a small bedroom with a bed, dresser and night stand. The log furniture and the quilt that covered the mattress fit the space perfectly.

"Thanks. The room is gorgeous."

"Glad you like it. The women at the church make the quilts and then auction them off at the annual Christmas Bazaar. If you're going to live here, you'll hear about it soon enough. Do you sew?"

Jess shook her head. "Not a stitch."

Justin laughed at her quip. "They'll change that, just you wait and see."

"They are more than welcome to try. My grandmother tried to teach me to crochet, but it never quite caught on." They were now standing inside the small bedroom. She couldn't help but admire how big and strong this man looked next to her. She was 5'6" in height, a nice normal height in her opinion. Not too short to reach things on the top shelf. And not so tall that she couldn't get away with wearing heels.

But compared to him, she was a dwarf. Justin was easily 6'4", maybe even 6'5" in height. He had broad shoulders, but a trim waist. He had removed his outer winter gear while she'd been cleaning up and now wore well-worn blue jeans with a navy blue flannel shirt.

The sound of a door shutting had Justin turning his head towards the sound. "That must be Kaillar. Want to come meet him?"

Jess was so tired and she could feel her energy slipping away. "Maybe tomorrow?"

Justin searched her eyes, seeing that the day had taken its toll on her. "Of course. Get some sleep, alright?"

"I will." She watched him turn to leave, stopping him at the doorway. "Justin…?"

"Yes?" He turned back into the room.

"Thank you."

He searched her eyes, looking to see what might be going through her lovely mind. "For what? We've already talked about me finding you."

"I know," she nodded. "Thank you for restoring my faith in humanity. It's been a while since someone did something nice for me without wanting something in return."

"That's too bad. You'll find the people of Silver Springs live to do nice things for people. We're like one big family here."

Jessica smiled tiredly. "Family sounds nice."

Justin looked like he wanted to say something, but then he cleared his throat and nodded in her direction. "You're more than welcome. See you in the morning."

Jess watched the door close behind him and then sprawled onto the quilt on the bed. Justin had offered her kindness because it was the right thing to do. And he hadn't expected anything in return.

She lay there in the dark, trying to turn her mind off. Her forehead hurt, her shoulders were achy, and her heart was in a state of confusion. Over the last few hours, she'd been on a mental rollercoaster: thoughts of Jason and his betrayal. Of little Thomas and how short his life had been. Of her grandmother and everything she'd done for her granddaughter; but the happy thoughts were overshadowed by the knowledge that she would never talk with her grandmother again.

And then there were the various emotions associated with being here in Silver Springs. Thankfulness that she'd been rescued from the mountain road. Excitement and trepidation over her new job. And a sense of curiosity about the man who'd taken her into his home and made her feel important. As if she mattered in this world. That feeling alone was addictive to her, and as she closed her eyes and drifted to sleep, she lectured herself about not falling back into her destructive patterns. It was time to stand on her own two feet; time to try and figure out what kind of person she wanted to be.

She wondered what advice her grandmother would have given her in dealing with Jason and her future. No doubt, it would have included reading her Bible, spending time in prayer, and finding a church to attend – all things she'd grown up doing regularly, but what had that ever gotten her?

She'd spent years trying to follow the rules. She'd been the recipient of more judgments from well-meaning parishioners than most kids her age. They'd either pitied her for having grown up without her parents, or they had summarily judged her unworthy and lacking in some way. She'd heard more than once that she wasn't living up to her parents' memory. What those self-righteous women didn't know, is that they had more memories of her parents than she did!

She removed the borrowed shirt and sweatpants, slipping beneath the covers and feeling her exhausted body sink down into the soft mattress. She immediately closed her eyes and a sigh of relief leaving her mouth. She was warm, safe, and that was all that mattered in that moment. Everything else could wait until the morning.

Chapter 7

Justin closed the door to the guest bedroom and leaned against the wall in the hallway. Jessica's words had gripped his heart and he'd had the strongest urge to pull her into his arms and offer her the comfort of a hug.

It's been a long time since someone has done something nice for me without wanting something in return.

How could that be? From what he could tell, she was a beautiful young woman who had chosen one of the most noble of professions – teaching. And yet, he sensed a sadness and anger in her that didn't make any sense. He had a strong urge to help her. He tried to convince himself it was purely platonic, but he couldn't get the smell of her perfume out of his head. Or how her hair looked so soft. He'd wanted to reach out and touch it.

But all of that he pushed aside as he replayed their conversations. There had been something in her voice when she'd mentioned her parents.

"Hey, where's she at?" Kaillar asked, coming around the corner to where Justin was.

Justin pushed away from the wall. "Calling it a night. She's exhausted. Dark circles under her eyes that go beyond the stress of today."

"How's her head?"

"She's gonna be bruised for a while. Her eye will probably be black and blue by tomorrow morning. She hit the back of that truck pretty hard, and the airbags in the steering wheel didn't deploy."

Kaillar raised a brow. "She's lucky she's alive!"

"Yeah. So..." Justin rolled his shoulders. "Is it still snowing?"

Kaillar nodded his head. "I almost stayed in town myself. That second hairpin curve was downright scary tonight."

Justin looked at him. "You okay?"

"Fine. The tracker's fine as well."

"Good. I better call Jeremy and let him know everything's okay. I also think I'll suggest they cancel basketball practice tomorrow morning."

"That'd be a good idea. No sense in people getting out if they don't have to."

Justin nodded. "I'll suggest he make phone calls tonight. It's only 8:30 p.m., most people will still be awake." He pulled his cell phone from his pocket and dialed the pastor's number, walking to the large picture windows and watching the snow fall as he waited for the call to connect.

"Justin?"

"Yeah, it's me. Just wanted to let you know everyone's safe and sound."

"Very good."

"I also think it might be wise to cancel practice tomorrow morning," Justin suggested.

"Already ahead of you. I made the calls about two hours ago."

Justin smiled and then sobered. "Did you know the school board hired a new elementary teacher?"

"I did. A young woman from somewhere out West, I believe."

"That's who I rescued this evening."

"Really? Well, I look forward to meeting her. Is she staying at Sarah's?"

"No, she bumped her forehead pretty good and I didn't want her spending the night alone. I brought her back to the lodge with me. Between Kaillar and me, we'll check on her through the night just to make sure she doesn't have any negative side effects."

"Why do I sense there is something else you want to say?" Pastor Jeremy told him.

"I had a chance to talk with her for a bit tonight. I sense she is very troubled, angry even, about events that happened in her past."

"And this bothers you?" Jeremy asked, intuitive as always.

"Yeah. I guess it does. She seems kind of alone and maybe a bit lost. I was wondering if you might talk to her?"

The pastor was quiet for a moment and then he offered some advice: "Justin, I am always available to talk to those in need. But might I suggest you stop trying to figure out what is wrong with her, and just be her friend? You've only just met her, and while I'm not discounting what you're sensing about her, she's new to town and a friend will mean much more than a counselor."

Justin smiled. "Point taken. I just don't like seeing her hurting. There's more to her than meets the eye."

"Justin, you are one of the best men I know. I cannot think of a man better suited to befriending a new member of our community. Just be careful that your motivation is in the right place."

"I get where you're going with this. I would never want to do anything that might make it harder for her to be here in Silver Springs. I'm just concerned that she needs help."

"So, no romantic interest there at all?" Jeremy asked. He was about the same age as Justin, having graduated from the high school in Silver Springs the same year. But while Justin had been busy flying around the skies, Jeremy had attended Bible school in the Midwest and married the love of his life. Lacy was a sweet girl and had fit into their little community without even trying.

Justin paused before answering. *Had he noticed how beautiful Jessica was? Yes! Most definitely. Especially after bringing her back to the lodge and getting to know her a bit.* "She's gorgeous. And I enjoyed talking with her, but she's troubled. I don't know that I can help her with whatever's bothering her, but I can't seem to let it go either. I feel compelled to try and help her, while she's here."

"Don't worry about that being a short amount of time. Paul Sherman told me she signed a two-year contract, so she's going to be here for a while. Why don't you bring her into town tomorrow afternoon and introduce her around? I'm sure Lacy will want to have her over for dinner, and you and your brothers are welcome to join us as well."

Justin smiled. "I never turn down Lacy's cooking, but I would imagine Kai and Mason will have other things to do. How about I bring her in after breakfast in the morning? I can drive her down in one of the trackers and that will give her time to figure out where she's going to stay."

"Didn't you hear? Part of her contract is a lease on the old Williams place. Jeff was back here a few weeks ago and has decided to stay in New York. His wife's doing well and he told Shirley down at the real estate office to start renting the place out. They left all of their furniture here as well."

Chapter 8

In fact, Justin hadn't been made aware of that information. "I hadn't heard that Jeff was back in Silver Springs."

"Yes, I believe that's when you and your brothers were escorting that group of archery hunters around in September."

"Not that it did any good. I am constantly amazed that intelligent men would pay thousands of dollars to come hunt in Colorado, and then not do everything they could to make sure they knew how to properly and accurately shoot their weapon of choice."

"I spoke with Kaillar last Sunday, and he made it seem as if the hunter had purchased the bow from a retail shop in Denver right before driving to meet you."

"That's about what it seemed like. He had this bag of accessories, none of which had been opened. I spent two hours, opening morning, installing them before turning him loose to practice on a target Mason set up for him."

"Did the man get lucky enough to hit anything?"

"That man couldn't hit the broad side of a barn if he was standing right in front of it. He was a terrible shot, and by his own admission, hadn't ever shot a bow and arrow before coming to see us."

"Makes a good case for making out-of-state hunters pass a basic test, doesn't it?" Jeremy chuckled and then continued, "Well, to summarize: the school board agreed to provide her with adequate housing for the first two years of her contract. They leased the Williams property the day before Jeff went back to New York."

"Well, living just a block away from the school will be very convenient."

"Is her car in need of being towed? I could call Frank over at the garage in the morning and have him go get it?" Jeremy offered.

"I'm not sure how bad the damage is, but that would be neighborly."

"Consider it done. Well, I better get off the phone and go help Lacy put the little ones back to bed."

Justin smiled. "Don't spoil them too much." Jeremy was the proud papa of twin boys. They were almost six-years-old and had started kindergarten this year. They were a handful at their best, and little terrors the rest of the time. But no-one seemed to mind overly much because they were so precocious about being naughty.

Justin thought back to this summer when the church had finished the new baptismal font. It was constructed so that it could be used both indoors or in the open air. Their daddy had filled it with water the day before he was going to use it and then turned on the heater, not wanting to freeze his parishioners when they were dunked beneath the water's surface.

Peter and James had attempted to save the native population of the local pond. They'd used their granddaddy's long fishing net to capture as many frogs as possible. Then they'd released them into the baptismal font and shut the lid.

When their father had gone to check the water temperature a few hours later, he'd lifted the lid and been accosted by eight very indignant frogs. Justin briefly wondered how Jessica would handle the twins. Silver Springs was so small that the elementary classes were combined with one another.

Kindergarten through second grade met together, third through fifth met together, sixth through eighth met in the middle school building. The high schoolers had their own building and several neighboring mountain communities bused their high school students in each day.

That meant that Jessica would soon find herself teaching a very rambunctious group of youngsters, of which Peter and James would be her most challenging.

"Do us a favor and don't forewarn the new teacher about the boys?" Jeremy pleaded with a laugh.

"Oh, I wouldn't dream of doing that. In fact, I think we should let her meet the boys tomorrow and see how well they get on," Justin suggested.

Jeremy's laugh got louder. "We'll see how they're acting tomorrow. I would hate for her to turn around and go back to Arizona without even giving one day in the classroom a shot."

"Your kiddos aren't that bad?" Justin assured him.

Jeremy groaned. "You say that because you do not have to constantly deal with their mischief."

"They'll grow out of it…"

"…and into what? That has both Lacy and I scared. If they're this hard to deal with at six, what are they going to be like at fourteen?"

"My uncle always had a remedy for horsing around and juvenile hijinks, as he called them. Hard work and lots of it."

"Good, thanks for volunteering. I'll be sending them you're way when the time comes," Jeremy assured him.

"Me and my big mouth. Have a good night and we'll see you sometime tomorrow around mid-morning."

"Later."

Justin pocketed his phone and then joined Kaillar in the kitchen. "Jeremy's threatening to send his little hooligans our way when they become teenagers."

Kaillar looked at him and then smiled. "We'll probably need some ditches dug then, don't you think?"

Justin smiled, remembering the summer he'd turned fifteen. He'd gotten his driving permit and was just a bit too big for his britches. Uncle Jed had decided that all of the ditches along the fence line needed to be cleaned out, deepened and then the weeds burned out of them.

It had taken Justin and his brothers the entire summer from sunrise to sundown, with only a few days off here and there. He'd never thought to complain about the extra work, and by the time the school year started again, he was back to being his usual self. His attitude of self-importance had disappeared in the smoke of the burning ditches.

In return, his uncle had gifted him his old Chevy pickup, and Justin had proudly driven his brothers to school during his junior and senior years.

"Where'd you go?" Kaillar asked.

"Just a quick turn down memory lane." Justin's face told more than his words did, and he saw Kaillar nod his head in full agreement.

"Do you still miss him?" Kaillar asked.

Justin nodded his head. "Every day." He looked up and then smiled. "But I think he's looking down and he's proud of us."

"I hope so," Kaillar agreed. "I really do."

Chapter 9

The next morning, Justin and Kaillar were sitting at the table when Jessica emerged from the guest room. "Good morning," Justin called to her. She looked marginally better, but a large purple and green bruise marred her forehead. Her eye was beginning to blacken, and he wondered if she'd looked in the mirror this morning, and if not, what her reaction to her appearance would be.

In his experience, most women were vain on some level. There wasn't anything she could do to make her injury disappear, but he figured she would still be upset over it and bemoan the fact.

"Hi," she offered softly, eyeing Kaillar curiously.

"Hey, I'm Kaillar. You were already turned in when I got back last night. That's a nice shiner you've got going there."

Justin smacked his brother on the back of the head. "Way to go, bro. Tact and manners get left on the mountain last night?"

"Sorry," Kaillar mumbled, watching Jessica for a negative reaction.

"Don't be mad at him for speaking the truth. I imagine I'm going to look like I went three rounds in the ring before the day is out."

"It's not that bad," Justin insisted.

"Thanks for trying to help, but to tell you the truth – a bruised forehead and black eye seem pretty insignificant compared to what could have happened if you all hadn't come out and rescued me."

"Our pleasure," Kaillar told. "How about some breakfast?"

Jessica joined them at the table. "That sounds really good." She watched as Kaillar got up from the table and placed a skillet on the stovetop. "Do you all know how to cook?"

"Yes, ma'am." When she frowned, he paused to ask, "What?"

"Well, ma'am makes me feel really old, and I'm probably not much older than you are."

"She's got you there."

Kaillar acknowledged that with a grin and a nod of his head. "Says the old man."

Justin looked offended and Jessica giggled. Justin turned to look at her, and was amazed at how the happiness seemed to transform her face. She'd just gone from gorgeous to breathtaking. Her eyes were bright, the green sparkling in the morning light that shone through the windows. Her blonde hair was pulled back into a ponytail, but her bangs hung across her forehead, and he had the strangest urge to brush them aside.

He let his gaze travel over her features – the slightly upturned nose, the pink lips that were only slightly chapped, and the light blush that stained her cheeks. This morning she looked healthy and so different from the woman he'd rescued last night, he was wondering if he'd imagined the hidden pain inside of her.

Justin felt his brother's eyes on him and he looked up, seeing the knowing smirk in Kaillar's eyes. Justin ignored the look and turned back to Jessica. "After breakfast, I told Jeremy I would bring you into town."

"Jeremy?" Jessica asked.

"Jeremy is the local preacher. He and his wife have a set of twin boys…"

"You'll be getting to know them rather well. They just entered kindergarten," Kaillar told her.

"I had a set of twin girls in my last classroom. They were so sweet." When both men started laughing, trying to contain it, but failing miserably, she looked at them and asked, "What's so funny?"

Kaillar got his control back first. "Sweet is not an adjective I would ever use to describe the Phillips twins."

"Oh, I'm sure we'll get along just fine. Do you think the roads will be clear enough to go and retrieve my car today?" she asked Justin.

"Frank is going to haul it back. The front end was pretty damaged." Seeing her curious look, he explained, "Frank owns the only gas station and automobile garage in Silver Springs. He's a crack mechanic and the only one with a tow truck nearby."

"So, he's going to get my car?"

"He is. He'll take a look at the damage and then get in touch with you. I also understand that you're going to be living in the Williams house. I'll take you over there and you can get settled."

"I spoke with someone from the school board and they told me the house was completely furnished."

"Yes. It is. I think you'll probably find everything you need there, but if there's anything you don't have, I'm sure the ladies at the church will be able to help you out."

Jessica firmed her lips and nodded. "I'm sure if there's anything I need I can do without it until I have a chance to do some shopping."

"I assure you the ladies in the church will count it an honor to help…"

Jessica shook her head. "I don't really plan on having much to do with the church, so to allow them to help me would feel like I was taking advantage of their generosity."

She doesn't plan on having much to do with the church? "You didn't even ask which church I was talking about."

"Is there more than one in town?" Jessica asked.

"Well, not really, but you sounded pretty absolute about the church."

Jessica shrugged her shoulders. "Not everyone is enthralled with the idea of religion. It's not that I'm an atheist or anything, but in my experience, God doesn't always play fair."

"How can you say that?" Kaillar asked her from the other side of the kitchen.

"I can say that because I've seen firsthand how God works. My parents were a great example." *And Thomas. And Jason's betrayal.* She didn't need any more examples. Those were more than enough to her way of thinking.

"Example of what?" Kaillar asked.

"Of how God plays favorites and following him only leads to heartache and pain."

"I think maybe you're looking at your situation from the wrong perspective. If anyone has reason to be mad at God, it would be me, Kaillar and Mason. Our mother was more interested in getting her next fix than she ever was in being a mother. And for someone who didn't want the responsibilities of parenthood, she didn't do much to prevent getting pregnant either."

"Yeah, Maria Donnelly probably counts as the worst mother in the world."

Jessica looked between the two men, "And yet you don't seem to have written God off."

"No, we're thankful that He allowed our uncle to become our guardian. Without Uncle Jed's influence and teaching, none of us would have made it to where we are now. The only way to explain how all three of us are still here, and weren't born addicted to drugs, or even aborted, is God. He intervened in a miraculous way, but ultimately our mother couldn't break free from the addictions that plagued her."

"That's so sad. So, do any of you know who your father is?"

Justin looked at her. "No. So, in that way, you are much better off than we are. I imagine you have stories from family and friends about your parents, pictures, and maybe even mementos.

"The only pictures and mementos we have from our mother were of when she was a young girl. Her parents were very against her move to California and then Las Vegas. They never understood what was driving her, and later, when it became apparent that drugs were her driving force, they couldn't deal with it."

"That's so sad," Jessica told them both.

"Don't feel sorry for us," Kaillar urged her, setting a fluffy omelet in front of her. "Uncle Jed was the best father we could ever have wanted. Just like parents who adopt their children, biology is only a piece of the puzzle when it comes to parenthood. Legacy. Heritage. Beliefs and traditions. Those types of things help, but again they don't make a family. Only love can do that."

Chapter 10

Kaillar's comment, about his parents, stuck with Jessica through the rest of the day. Right after she'd finished eating a wonderful breakfast, Justin had lent her a leather and fleece-lined coat. It was rather large on her, but once they'd stepped outside and she realized how cold it really was, she was extremely grateful.

"I'm going to have to get some warmer clothing."

"Well, there's a small shop in town that sells some things, but you'll probably need to go into Silverthorne to find a better selection."

"I drove through a town called Vail just before I headed up the mountain."

Justin shook his head. "Well, I don't know about your finances, but the prices are definitely going to be much higher there."

Jessica gave a small laugh. "Where was that other place you mentioned?" In truth, she had a very nice pile of money sitting in her bank, but rather than go on a big shopping spree, she'd continued to live on what she could make, saving the money in the bank for a rainy day. Outfitting herself for life in the Colorado Mountains just might qualify as such a day!

Justin smiled. "About thirty minutes from here when the roads are cleared."

"That's not so far away. So, you're going to take me to meet..."

"Well, the preacher and his wife, and their two kids. We're having dinner with them later. Before then, I thought I'd just take you around and introduce you to whomever we meet."

"You know everyone in town?" Jessica asked, shocked at the idea.

"Well, I know most of the people who live in town. There are quite a number of people who live up in the mountains…"

"Like you?" Jessica asked, following him to the barn and watching as he climbed aboard one of the trackers.

"Yes, like me and my brothers. We've lived on this mountain since we came here to live with my uncle. He and our mother grew up here. Our great-great-grandparents were homesteaders and came here during the Colorado Gold Rush era."

"Gold? Did they ever find any?"

Justin nodded. "A bit, but never enough to open a mine."

"What do you do up here?" Jessica asked, climbing into the passenger seat.

"My brothers and I run an outfitting and guide service. During the fall, we mostly guide hunters. But as soon as the snow begins to melt, there will be a steady stream of hikers eager to conquer the 'fourteeners' of Colorado. There are five such peaks within an hours' drive from here. We also ski and make up the primary search and rescue team for these mountains."

"Wow! You guys stay busy," she commented softly.

Justin grinned at her. "We enjoy what we do so it doesn't always seem like work. Do you ski?"

Jessica laughed. "No! I don't really do anything athletic. I mean, I played a little softball when I was in school, but just for fun."

"We'll have to get you up on the slopes then. It won't be long now, not with storms like these helping out."

"I think I'll probably pass…"

"Nearly everyone around here skis. Jeff probably left both downhill and cross-country skis at the house. We'll check it out when I drop you off there later."

"Justin, I really think I'll pass. If downhill skiing is what I've seen on television, I can already tell you I will be the one rolling down the slope in a tangle of arms and legs. In fact, I would be the one setting off the avalanche."

"Firstly, you're probably referring to downhill racing, and while there are a few race courses at some of the other slopes, around here, most people just like to ski for fun. And cross-country skiing is kind of a must. Even your kindergartners will be able to move about the town on skis."

"No one said I needed to ski in order to teach…"

"You don't have to know how, but it will make getting around town much easier come January. The house the school board rented for you is only a block from the school. When there is several feet of snow on the road, skiing to school will look a whole lot more palatable than digging your car out so you can drive that one block."

"Silver Springs gets a lot of snow?" she asked in trepidation. She was definitely going to have to invest some money in her car. At the very least, she'd need to invest in some good snow tires. She grew quiet and looked around at the snow-covered trees, marveling at how crisp and clean everything looked in the light of a new day.

The skies had cleared of their storm clouds from the day before, and a brilliant blue sky could be seen through the branches of the trees. The air was crisp and clean, with no hint of smog or pollution, and a sense of peace seemed to fill her chest and expand to reach all of the dark corners.

"It's so beautiful," she murmured, mostly to herself, almost unaware of her companion.

Justin heard her soft comment and as they rounded the top of the next hill, he paused the tracker, giving her an overview of Silver Springs below and the surrounding mountains and valleys. He kept his voice low and his tone calm. "There's Silver Springs."

"It's like a picture out of some magazine. I can't believe places like this really exist."

"Believe it. Every time I see these mountains, I'm reminded of God's goodness and how magnificent his Creation truly is." Justin watched her and was shocked to see she wasn't denying either God or the concept of Creation. *So, what was it about God and church that she was so against?*

"I can't say I'm not nervous about the snow, but I'm so glad I'm here."

"Let's go see the town." Justin put the tracker in gear and slowly began their descent. The Three Brothers Lodge sat at approximately ninety-five hundred feet, with the town of Silver Springs about five hundred feet lower in elevation.

On either side of the town, magnificent mountains, their tops white with snow as they rose above the tree line, nestled the small community in their valley. As they drew closer, Jessica could begin to make out individual buildings: the school, the church, and what appeared to be Main Street. Very little movement was taking place in the small town, and she assumed that was in part due to the snow that had fallen overnight.

They passed the elementary school and she noticed the parking lot was empty. "No school today?" It was Thursday, and not a formal holiday that she was aware of. She wasn't scheduled to begin her new position until Monday, but she would have enjoyed popping in to observe her new students unawares.

"No. They cancelled it late yesterday afternoon. You'll find that happens quite often around here. The school year is built around a four-day school week, so during the months of August and September, the kids go five days a week, allowing for some extra snow days during the months of October through March."

"March! When exactly does the snow begin to melt around here?" she asked, trying to imagine living in snow for more than six months of each year.

"You look completely shocked," he commented with a soft chuckle. "It will be snowing around here until March. Maybe the first part of April. You'll get used to it, but by the time spring arrives, you'll be ready for it and summer to arrive."

"I'm not prepared for that much snow."

"How about we stop by the clothing store first then?" Justin suggested.

"I think that would be a very good idea." Jessica looked down at the borrowed, too-big coat, her one pair of jeans, her tennis shoes, and was glad that for the first time since her grandmother's death, she would have something to spend the money on that was left over from the sale of her grandmother's house. She would be able to buy whatever she needed, and for the first time ever, she wouldn't have to look at the price tags, or run a quick total in her head before approaching the checkout counter. She would be able to shop without worry, knowing that when the clerk rang up her purchases, she could simply write a check and know the funds were available.

Chapter 11

Chloe's General Store was much more than Jessica had hoped for. Justin escorted her inside the large building, waving to a dark-haired woman with glasses who stood behind the checkout counter. The woman was stunning in an almost ethereal way, and Jessica found that talking to the woman was easier than anything she'd ever done.

"Morning, Chloe."

"Hey, Justin! What brings you down the mountain this morning? Who's that with you?" The woman came out from behind the counter and Jessica watched as she waddled towards them. She was as big as a house with her pregnancy, and looked ready to deliver at any time.

"This is Jessica Andrews. Jessica, this vision is Chloe Taylor. Her husband Scott is the fire chief around here. Jessica is the new elementary teacher."

Chloe reached for Jessica's hand. "Hi! Welcome to town. We're so glad you're here. My mother has been tearing her hair out, literally. She'll be so relieved to have you here next week."

Jessica thought she was following the connection between Chloe and her mother, but she asked for clarification anyway. "Your mother is?"

"Shelly Downs. She's the school principal, and substitute teacher for the last three weeks."

Jessica nodded her head. "Do you mind me asking, what happened to the previous teacher?"

Chloe read her unspoken concern and smiled. "Nothing like you're thinking. Deidre moved to Colorado Springs to be with her husband. He's returning from Afghanistan on the thirtieth, and will be stationed there for the next two years of his life. "

"Well, I guess I'm happy that she gets to be with her husband, but I can imagine she was very sad to be leaving her small charges. I know how I felt leaving my classroom."

Chloe put her hands on her stomach and smiled. "This is our first child, but I already feel so connected to him. Do you have any children?"

"No," Jessica told her. She held up her left hand. "No husband. I'm probably a little old-fashioned in that way, but I truly believe a child needs two parents whenever possible."

"I agree with you." Chloe looked her up and down and then smiled. "You're here for some more appropriate clothing?"

"What was your first clue?" Jessica asked with a welcoming smile. The instant connection she felt to this woman was amazing. Jessica had never been able to communicate with someone she'd just met – not like she was communicating with the lovely Chloe. After Jason's betrayal, she'd distanced herself from everyone, not trusting herself to be a good judge of character any longer. *Maybe these people will be different.*

"The shoes were a dead giveaway. Come with me and we'll get you all fixed up." She looked at Justin. "She's in good hands if you have some other things to do."

Justin shook his head and held up his hands. "I get the message. I'll be over at the garage when you're through here."

"The garage?" Jessica asked, feeling a little nervous about him leaving her here by herself.

"Down the block on the corner. You can't miss it."

"Don't worry none. I'll make sure she gets there. Now, get out of here and let us get to work." Chloe shooed him away and then headed for the back of her store. "Come on back here. That's a nice coat, but a little big on you."

"Justin lent it to me. I guess I didn't really think my move through. I really didn't expect snow this soon." The more Jessica tried to defend coming to Colorado so unprepared, the more embarrassed she became.

Chloe saw that and hugged her with one arm. "Don't beat yourself up about it. It's not like they have much snow in Arizona. How about some hot chocolate?"

"To tell you the truth, before yesterday I'd never seen snow, let alone driven in it. It was really scary out there on the highway. I don't know how I'll ever repay Justin and his brothers for coming to find me. And I'd love some hot chocolate."

Chloe smiled. "That's what the Donnelly brothers do. Rescue people. Have you met the other two yet?"

Jessica shook her head as Chloe led her back to a small break room. "Just Kaillar. The other brother spent the night someplace called Frisco?"

She turned the electric tea kettle on and then handed Jessica a cup and a hot chocolate packet. "Sorry it's not homemade, but with the baby coming, and the holidays, who has time for things like that?"

"When are you due?" Jessica asked, stirring the powder into the hot water that had just been added to her cup.

"In four weeks! I can't believe it. Scott and I still have so much to do, and now with the weather getting bad, I don't know if we're going to get everything done." Chloe started pulling clothing off the hangars and dumping it into her arms.

"So, where exactly is Frisco?" Jessica, having meant to ask Justin earlier, but he wasn't around anymore.

"On the other side of the pass. Frisco's the closest place with a good-sized medical clinic and helicopter service into Denver or back to Junction. Of course there's always Vail, but most normal people avoid going there if they can. Too expensive and everyone seems to have their nose permanently fixed in the air."

"Snobs?" Jessica asked, trying to see Chloe above the mountain of clothes currently in her arms.

"The worst. Okay, that should give you a good start. If you'll just turn around, I'll open up the dressing room and you can get started. Toss out anything you want to keep, and just leave the rest on the hangar inside the cubicle."

"Chloe, how many clothes do you think I need?" Jessica asked as she dumped the pile of clothing onto the wooden bench inside the changing room.

"Well, you'll be teaching four days per week, and then there's outside activities, and church and…"

"No church. I don't attend."

Chloe looked at her. "What? But I thought I read somewhere that your parents were missionaries?" She was very confused, and didn't try to hide it.

Jessica swallowed. "Where did you read that?"

"The school board held a public meeting before they offered you the job. Your resume and bio was read by practically everyone in town."

Jessica sighed; she hadn't counted on that. She was trying to make a new start, and while she had accomplished her task of getting away from Jason, it seemed that her upbringing was now going to be the problem.

"My parents' viewpoints on religion aren't necessarily mine." Jessica pretended not to see the look of horror and then pity that crossed Chloe's face. Since becoming an adult, she'd done everything possible to ignore her heritage. Turning her thoughts to her reason for being in this store, she quickly tried on the clothing Chloe had piled into her arms and after half an hour, she'd found two pairs of jeans, some corduroy pants, three sweaters, and several turtle necks to wear beneath them.

When she emerged Chloe was beaming at her and had a selection of boots for her to try on. She had also located a sheepskin coat, very similar to the one that Justin had lent her, but this time the sleeves were just the right length, and as she tried it on, she couldn't help but enjoy the way the coat seemed to wrap her in comfort, giving her a sense of safety. *It's just a coat, Jess. Easy there.*

"So, I'll start ringing this up for you, shall I?" Chloe asked.

Jessica smiled and then nodded. "I'm not sure how to get all of this stuff…"

Chloe grinned. "Don't worry about it. We're actually going to be neighbors. We live right next to the Williams house."

"Really? That's wonderful. So, Justin told me your husband is a fireman?"

"Scott is sort of the head fireman in town. Not that we have a lot of house fires in town, but he and his crew are also trained forest fighters. With the recent beetle kill of the pine trees, the threat of a major fire disaster seems closer every year."

"It sounds like I have a lot to learn about Colorado. And here I was worried about teaching." Jessica laughed at herself and when Chloe joined in, she looked at the woman and knew they were going to be good friends.

Chapter 12

Four hours later, Jessica was getting out of Justin's tracker and looking in awe at what would be her new home for the next two years. The house was huge and magnificent, and looked so inviting and charming that Jessica couldn't believe she was going to be living there!

"Wow! How many people lived here?" Jessica asked Justin as he took her elbow and steadied her up the front walk. Someone had shoveled the snow off the concrete, and she was wearing her new snow boots, but she wasn't used to walking on icy surfaces and was still slipping around a bit.

"Easy! Jeff had four sisters and then their parents and his maternal grandmother all lived here."

"Eight people? No wonder the house is so huge. I can't possibly need this much space!"

Justin smiled at her as they reached the front door. "My suggestion is to pick out the rooms you want to use, and then close off the rest." He opened the door and gestured with his hand for her to precede him inside.

Jessica stomped the snow from her boots and stepped inside. The lights inside flared to life and she looked around at a beautifully decorated room. A large fireplace stood along the left wall and overstuffed couches sat across from each other in front of it, with several blankets and pillows tossed carelessly here and there.

Beyond that, she could see a large wooden table with benches instead of chairs, and she could already see herself cutting out bulletin board decorations on the large surface. The wooden floors showed years of wear, and the braided throw rugs reminded her of growing up with her grandmother.

"This place is lovely," she told Justin. She removed her coat and then her snow boots before venturing further into the room.

"There are three bedrooms downstairs. One of them is the suite that Jeff's grandmother used. It has a full bathroom and a walk-in closet."

"It sounds like I could easily live on the ground floor and never go upstairs."

Justin grinned. "Probably. Want to go take a look around first before you make your decision?"

Jessica smiled and nodded. She felt like a kid in a toy store. She'd never really had much choice when it came to where she was going to live. Her grandmother's house had been older with only one extra bedroom. Then she'd gone off to college and lived in the dorms.

During the two years she'd been out of college, she'd lived in a small studio walk-up a few blocks away from the college. Part of her graduate program was working part-time in a local elementary school. The extra income had enabled her to afford the extra cost, but it had been worth it to be away from the social atmosphere of the college campus.

She hadn't worried about how small the apartment had been because she'd spent so much of her time with Jason. He was actually from a town four hours away, but he'd only gone home every other week. He lived in a rented condo with plenty of room, and even though he'd tried to get her to move in with him, she'd maintained that she liked knowing she had her own space to retreat to.

That had been her best decision in the long run. One morning she'd come back from a teacher in-service to find a strange car parked outside his condo. She'd been expecting to see one of his friends from college had come to visit, or maybe his parents were visiting. She hadn't had a chance to meet them yet, but Jason had promised to make that a reality soon.

He'd not been in the living portion of the house, so she'd wrongly assumed that he'd left with his visitor. She'd headed into the master bedroom, intending to gather up the laundry and take advantage of a few hours off. But when she'd stepped inside, she'd immediately realized her mistake.

Jason had indeed been home, as had his visitor: a gorgeous redhead, with a body that models would die for, was sitting in the bed, straddling Jason's hips, and in the process of removing her clothing. A woman who had a very large diamond on her ring finger: Jason's fiancée!

She shook her head, trying to dispel the memories because they served no purpose except to remind her that she really shouldn't trust her own judgment. She'd trusted Jason and look what had happened. She been dating him for almost three years, and the entire time he'd been engaged to the redhead back home. The entire time!

She'd been humiliated more than heartbroken, and it disturbed her sense of self-confidence. In truth, getting used to being alone had been easier than dealing with the fact that Jacob had lied to her and she'd believed him!

"You okay there?" a voice behind her right shoulder asked.

She turned her head and nodded. "Sorry, I guess I was daydreaming."

Justin smiled at her. "Anything you want to talk about?"

Talk about? With you? Oh, no way! There is no way I want to demonstrate how stupid I was by talking with you about Jason! That is so not going to happen! Jessica hid her disquiet behind a shake of her head. "No, thanks, but I'd rather take a look around."

"Sure thing. Let's start upstairs."

Jessica nodded and climbed the narrow staircase, reinforcing in her mind that living downstairs was going to be her preference. The upstairs rooms were lovely, but the thought of climbing that staircase multiple times a day wasn't at all appealing.

"Ready to go see the downstairs?" Justin asked.

"Yes. I think I'll close these rooms up now. I would much rather live downstairs."

"Okay," Justin agreed, helping her turn the heat down and close the doors to the hallway.

"Why did you only turn the heat down instead of off?" Jessica asked as they descended the staircase.

"You don't want the water pipes to freeze. It's okay to turn the heat down, but you need to keep all areas of the house above freezing or you'll be waking up to broken pipes."

Jessica sighed. "Wonderful. Another perk of living in Colorado."

Justin laughed and started down the hallway. "You'll get used to the way we do things here sooner or later."

They finished their perusal of the downstairs, and Jessica fell in love with the large canopy bed, which occupied the mother-in-law suite on the main floor. "This is perfect for me," she told him.

He started to say something, but the front doorbell peeled through the house. "Want me to see who that is?"

Jessica nodded and followed behind him as they went to answer the door.

Justin pulled the door open to see Pastor Jeremy standing there, a large baking dish in his hands. "Hey! We were just getting ready to head your direction."

Jeremy stepped inside as Justin stepped back. "Don't bother. Both twins had pinkeye. Lacy just got back from Doc's with them. They're under quarantine until Monday, so she sent dinner over here."

He glanced around Justin and smiled. "Hi. I'm Jeremy Phillips, the pastor of Silver Springs Community Church. And the twins I mentioned will no doubt be your biggest challenge."

Jessica smiled. "I've found that big challenges also come with big rewards."

Jeremy smiled and then turned to Justin. "I like her optimism. I almost hate for her to meet Peter and James and dispel the myth."

Jessica laughed. "I'm sure we'll get along very well. But thank you for the heads up about the pinkeye. I'll have to check with the janitor and see that the room is disinfected prior to Monday's class. I've seen it spread through an entire classroom in just a few days."

"Well, Doc already contacted Shelley and I'm sure she's already got a handle on what needs to happen. Where can I set this down?"

Jessica led the way back to the kitchen and then listened in for several minutes as Justin and Jeremy spoke about a basketball team and several other items of business. The rapport the two had was amazing, considering one of them was a pastor. He seemed so down to earth, and unlike the pastor she'd grown up knowing, he didn't come off as holier than thou or self-righteous. It was almost enough to have her second-guessing her decision to steer clear of the local church crowd. Almost.

Chapter 13

One week later...

Jessica had just sent the last of her students out the door with her parents, and she slumped into her chair and let her head fall into her hands. She was exhausted, and felt so relieved that today marked the end of her first week in Silver Springs Elementary School. She could have cried.

Handling twenty children wasn't normally a problem for her, with or without a classroom aid. But these twenty children seemed to have the energy of two hundred!

The Phillips twins were by far the instigators, even though they were some of the youngest in the classroom. Peter and James seemed to be wherever trouble was to be found, but their explanations for doing whatever it was they'd done was so well thought out and, to the mind of a six-year-old, logical, that Jessica had been hard-pressed to discipline them for most of their antics.

She'd begun to feel more comfortable in the small community, with Chloe becoming her champion. The woman had arrived each afternoon with some new place to show her. The only day she hadn't spent some time with the woman had been Sunday. Chloe had urged her to attend the morning service with her and her husband, but Jessica had remained fixed in her denial. Instead, she'd spent the morning cleaning her new home from top to bottom, at least the rooms she was using, and then walked down through the town, making note of the various businesses that existed so close to home.

Since it was Sunday she'd been able to window browse without having to deal with the owners of each business. She'd arrived back home a few minutes before noon, planned so that she wouldn't run the risk of seeing all the people filing out of the small church.

She heard her classroom door open and looked up to see Principal Shelley Downs step into the room. "Hi."

She looked at Jess and then laughed. "Oh, my dear. If you could see your face... I just came by to congratulate you on surviving week one. I promise the following weeks will be easier."

"I sure hope so. Since you're here, could you explain what's happening with the Christmas Pageant?"

Shelley pulled up another adult-sized chair. "Sure. It's kind of a big thing here in Silver Springs. The entire community comes out for it. We'll have a full Nativity scene; some of the local men made wooden cutouts of the animals years ago and the middle schoolers are going to repaint them in the next few weeks.

"Each classroom will choose several songs to sing, or maybe even a small skit. Lacy Phillips usually comes in and helps with that portion of the pageant. She has a wonderful voice and directs the children's choir at the church."

"Okay, I'll contact her..."

"You could probably just talk to her at church this Sunday," Shelley suggested.

Jessica felt uncomfortable and then shook her head. "I probably won't attend."

Shelley looked at her and then sighed. "Okay, explain to me how the daughter of missionaries doesn't want to attend church."

Jessica had come to respect Shelley over the last four days, and felt herself drawn to open up to the older woman. "Look, I realize that you and most of this town feel that God is good, and He takes care of His people. But in my experience, that's not the way it works."

"Because your parents were murdered?"

Jessica sighed. "You read my bio too?" When Shelley nodded her head, Jessica cringed. "Well, yes! I blame God for sending them back into such a dangerous place."

Shelley looked at her with compassion in her eyes. "But so much good came from that situation." When Jessica simply looked at her, Shelley pulled out her tablet and typed a few search words into it. When she found what she was looking for, she handed the tablet to Jessica and told her, "Read."

Jessica took the tablet and read a news story from more than twenty years earlier. It was a story about how the Christians in South Africa had risen up against the terror groups threatening to exterminate them.

The people being interviewed credited the missionaries and their families for showing them what true leadership was, that there was no sacrifice too great when spreading the love of Christ.

Jessica handed the tablet back, feeling her old anger issues rise to the surface. "Is that supposed to make it all better? It doesn't. And my parents aren't the only ones He's let down." She explained to Shelley about Thomas, but couldn't bring herself to admit her failure with Jason.

Shelley opened her mouth to reply, but a tap on the classroom door had both women turning to welcome Justin. Jessica hadn't seen him since Saturday when he'd brought over the box from her vehicle. She smiled at him, pleased to see him and get a reprieve from where the conversation with Shelley was headed. "Hi!"

"Hope I'm not interrupting anything?" he asked, walking inside and joining them by Jessica's desk.

Jessica shook her head, a little too eagerly. "No, in fact, we were just finishing. What are you doing here?"

"Well, Mason's cooking tonight and I thought you might like to join us. I'm interested to hear how your first week went."

Jessica knew she should decline his offer. Her mind had strayed to thoughts of the handsome man more than once this past week, but the thought of returning home with her emotions still churned up from her conversation with Shelley wasn't pleasant. "I'd love to. Let me get the classroom cleaned up and I'll be ready to go."

"Frank said to tell you he'll have the parts to fix your vehicle early next week."

"Great! Not that I'm planning to do much driving."

Shelley watched the interaction between the two and then stood up. "I'm going to get out of your hair. Think about what I said," she told Jessica, concern in her voice.

Jessica swallowed. "I will. Have a nice weekend." She turned away and began gathering up the art supplies scattered across the classroom.

"Justin, since you're here, would you mind helping me change the light in my office? It went out first thing this morning and Tim didn't have a chance to change it yet. I was hoping to get some more work done on next year's budget, but that won't happen without light."

Justin smiled. "I'd be happy to. Be right back," he told Jessica. He followed Shelley out into the hall, having picked up on the fact that she just wanted a chance to talk to him. Once they were several doors down the hallway, she stopped and faced him.

"What are you doing?"

Justin was taken aback. "What are you talking about?"

"Don't mess with my new teacher. She's really good with the kids, and I really feel that God sent her here for a reason that has nothing to do with her students."

Justin grinned. "Don't worry so much. I got to know her a bit last week and would like to know her even more. She's a nice girl..."

"With some real anger problems. Mostly directed at God."

"What were you two discussing when I arrived?" Justin wore a concerned expression, and snippets of previous conversations with Jessica flowed through his mind.

"Her parents. I think she blames God for their deaths, and has let her anger color every aspect of her life. And there was a young man who died young and she blames God for that as well."

"Yeah, I kind of picked up on that too. Want me to talk to her?"

"Only if you get the chance. She wants nothing to do with the church and I'm worried that she's denying an integral part of herself. I guess I'm playing mother here, but there's something about Jessica that makes me want to help her."

Justin knew exactly what Shelley was talking about. He'd gotten the same feeling when he'd been showing Jessica around the town on the previous Friday. Silver Springs was such a small community, and most people were involved in the church in some way. Even those who lived in the surrounding mountains tried to attend Sunday services at least once a month.

Justin had encouraged her to re-think her position on becoming involved in the church, promising that no-one was going to pressure her to do anything other than attend, but she'd been pretty adamant about wanting to keep her distance. "I'll see what I can do."

He left Shelley in the hallway and returned to Jessica's classroom. She was just picking up her coat, and he walked across and held it out for her to put her arms in. Without thinking about his actions, he scooped her hair out of the neck, lifting it up and allowing his fingertips to just barely graze the bare skin at the back of her neck.

She shivered in reaction, and he felt the strongest urge to wrap his arms around her and hold her close. He pushed the urge aside as he dropped her hair and stepped back. She spun around and looked at him, and he could see her reaction had taken her as much by surprise as his own had.

"Ready to go?"

"Sure. I need to swing by the house and change my clothes first."

"We can do that. I have the truck today since the snow has begun to melt off the roads."

They stepped out of the school and he led her to his big, black double cab truck. There were steps by the passenger door, and she knew without them she wouldn't have been able to scramble up into it without his help.

"You alright there?" he asked, smiling at her as she settled into the seat.

"What's with the monster truck?" she asked with a grin.

"Feet of snow, remember? This rig gets me just about anywhere I need to go where roads are involved. I spent many years in my late teens digging the tires of my uncle's old Chevy pickup out of the snow. With this *monster* as you called it, I just put it in gear and drive."

Jessica smiled as she watched him talk about his truck. He had such a boyish enthusiasm for the subject, and she found she really liked seeing him smile and laugh. *Had Jason ever laughed like that? Or at himself?*

As the afternoon and evening progressed, Jessica found herself comparing the two men more often than not. At every turn, Justin came out the winner. By the time he drove her back down the mountain, she was more than a little enamored of the man who seemed intent on being her friend.

It didn't help that Chloe was constantly singing Justin's praises. He was best friends with her husband Scott, and she was just sure that Jessica and Justin would make a wonderful couple. Jessica had tried to let Chloe know that she really wasn't in a position to even think about a new relationship, but without going into Jason's betrayal, her protests sounded weak.

So, you happen to like what you know about Justin. Maybe you should give romance one more try and see if you can't restore your faith in your own judgment at the same time.

Jessica wasn't quite sure what was up with her inner voices, but ever since arriving in Silver Springs they had been more vocal than ever. Her inner voices had even begun to sound a bit like her beloved grandmother, urging her not only to give herself a chance to rebuild her faith, but to give God another chance. Everything had happened for a purpose, and even though Jessica knew the words to be true deep down, on the surface she was having trouble letting go of the hurt and disappointment of the past.

Chapter 14

Saturday morning...

Jessica stretched and tried to figure out what had woken her up. It was Saturday and she had made a point of turning her alarm clock off the night before. *So what...?*

A knock sounded on the front door again and she groaned, "Go away!" Knowing they couldn't hear her, she stumbled from the bed, pulling her bathrobe on as she headed for the front door. The wooden floors were chilly, reminding her she'd forgotten her slippers.

She pulled the door open, blinking into the bright sunshine.

"Good morning! Ready to go have some fun?" Justin asked cheerfully from the porch.

"What? Do you know what time it is?" she asked, rubbing the sleep from her eyes and hoping her hair wasn't standing up all over her head.

Justin chuckled. "Someone's not a morning person, I see."

"No! Someone was sleeping in for the first time in... I can't even remember the last time I slept in. Not to be rude, but what do you want?"

Justin stepped into the house, forcing her to back up or risk getting her bare toes stepped on. "You are going to learn to cross-country ski today."

Jessica shook her head. "No way! I am going back to my nice, warm bed. But you go ahead and knock yourself out." She made to turn away, but she tripped on the belt of her robe. Her feet slid on the wooden floors, and she would have fallen backwards, had Justin not been so quick to react.

He grabbed her by the waist, lifting her off her feet and then holding her against his chest. "Whoa! You need to be more careful."

Jessica felt his arms around her waist and had the strongest urge to lay her head upon his chest and just absorb his warmth. Instead, she pushed away from him, gaining her feet beneath her and hurriedly backing away from him. "Sorry."

"Look, most of the town will be at the hill this morning."

"The hill?" Jessica questioned him with a raised brow.

"Just on the other side of town there is a moderate hill the locals use to teach their children to ski. There are also cross-country trails that begin and return there."

"I really just want to go back to bed," Jessica told him.

"Well, I have appointed myself your social director and I say you need to learn to cross-country ski. We're going to get more snow this coming week, and skiing to school will be easier than trying to walk through two feet of snow."

"We're going to get two feet of snow?" she asked, looking out the window at the sunshine currently being displayed.

"That's what they're forecasting. We'll probably get more, but it won't be a big deal if you know how to ski."

Jessica sighed. "You're not going to go away until I agree, are you?"

Justin crossed his arms over his chest and shook his head. "Nope. Might as well give in and I'll let you have the cinnamon roll from Becky's bakery, sitting in my truck along with a fresh cup of coffee."

Jessica groaned. "You don't play fair." Becky owned the small bakery in town, and Jessica had tasted her creations firsthand at the school.

"Gotcha. Go get dressed in something warm and I'll go dig the skis out of the garage."

"Fine. But I want my cinnamon roll now."

Justin laughed but went back to the truck and returned with a bag containing the cinnamon roll and a cardboard cup of coffee. "Now, will you please go and get dressed?"

Jessica took the food and wandered back down the hallway, sipping the coffee as she went. She pulled a pair of jeans from the closet, and then added a turtleneck and a sweater. She donned her snow boots, and pulled her hair back into a sloppy ponytail. She didn't worry about makeup, figuring the cold air would provide a natural blush to her cheeks in short order.

Justin was waiting for her on the front porch and she grabbed her coat before closing the door. She still had half of her cinnamon roll, and she ate it as Justin drove them out of town.

The hill became visible almost immediately, cluttered with townspeople, and Jessica immediately wished she hadn't let Justin talk her into doing this. "I don't really need to learn to ski."

"Of course you do. Look," he pointed out the window as he parked the truck. "There's Jeremy and Lacy."

Jessica turned on him. "You expect me to learn to ski where my students can see me fail?"

"You're not going to fail, and believe me, Peter and James will be too busy driving their parents crazy to notice something like their teacher falling in the snow. Besides, I'm a really good teacher, and if you just trust me, I promise to keep you from falling."

Jessica heard his words, but her mind immediately added a double meaning to them. He was watching her so intently, it was almost as if he truly meant them in more than one way. She watched him remove the skis from the back of the truck and then he came around and showed her how to adjust the buckles to fit the ski boots he'd also found hidden in the garage.

Once done, he changed into his own ski gear and then helped her out of the truck. "Okay, so the toe of each boot is attached to the ski, allowing you to lift your heel as you bend your knee." He demonstrated the movement that would allow her to push her skis forward without picking them up off the snow.

"Now, you try it."

Justin was about ten feet away, and Jessica looked around her, pleased to see that absolutely no-one was paying any attention to her. Taking a deep breath, she released it. "Okay, you can do this. How hard can it be?" She mimicked his movement, giving a short squeak of alarm when her body moved forward.

"That's it. Now repeat the motion with the other foot."

Jessica did as he requested and a moment later, she was standing by his side. She grinned up at him. "I did it!"

"Yes, you did. Let's go try one of the easier trails. We don't want to go too far today, or you'll hate me in the morning." He pushed off and she was left trying to keep up with him.

When he took a break a few moments later, she asked, "Why am I going to hate you tomorrow?"

"Well…you're using muscles that probably haven't been used like this before. You're going to be a little sore."

"Great!" she told him, her voice full of sarcasm.

"Still want to go on?"

"I'm already out here now. Might as well."

"There's that burst of enthusiasm I was waiting for," he commented with a wry grin.

Jessica laughed. "Listen, you dragged me from a warm bed, put these tiny sleds on my feet, and also expect me to be jumping for joy? That might be expecting a little too much."

Justin held out his ski pole to her. "Grab hold." When she did, he pulled her up so that she was by his side. "With you, I might expect a whole lot of things. But never too much." His tone had softened and Jessica found herself unable to look away from his eyes.

After a moment, common sense tried to intervene and she whispered, "Justin, what's going on here?"

He looked into her eyes and then smiled. "I don't know, but it could be fun finding out. Don't you think?"

Jessica returned his smile, the day too beautiful to allow memories of past disappointments to overshadow the promise of the future. "I want to believe that, I really do…"

"That's all it takes. Just a little belief. A little faith. Give whatever this is between us a chance. I've felt it since the moment I woke you up on the mountain."

"I've felt it as well, but my last relationship almost destroyed me."

Justin lifted a hand and brushed a stray piece of hair back behind her ear. "Why don't we finish the short loop and then head back to your place. I think maybe it's time we talked more about our past histories." When she tried to shake her head, he tapped her on the nose. "No pressure, only what you want to share. I want to know more about you. You said you came to Colorado to make a fresh start. I want to be part of that."

Jessica looked at him and then slowly nodded her head. "I think maybe I'd like that as well."

Justin winked at her and then used her grip on his ski pole to push her behind him. "Let's finish this track, and then go shopping. I'm cooking tonight."

Jessica giggled. "That's a really good thing since I am an absolutely horrible cook." She followed behind him, and by the time they returned to his truck her muscles were shrieking at her in protest. Something told her she was going to be more than sore come morning.

Chapter 15

Justin put the finishing touches on the steaks and then stuck them back under the broiler. "Won't be long now, do you want butter and sour cream on your potato?"

Jessica wandered into the kitchen. "Sure. Do you want to eat at the table or by the fireplace?"

"Fireplace gets my vote."

"Great. I'll go put the silverware and our drinks on the coffee table."

Justin watched her gather up forks and knives and then two glasses of ice water. She'd been acting more nervous as the day wore on. He figured it had to do with whatever had driven her from Arizona in the first place.

He didn't want her nervous, but if she couldn't learn to trust him, to listen and not pass judgment, they really didn't have much of a future together. That was not something he even wanted to consider at the present time.

They carried their plates to the living room and ate in silence for several minutes before Jessica moaned. "Justin, this is amazing! If I ate like this all the time I'd be as big as a house!"

Justin shook his head. "No, you wouldn't. And you could put on a few pounds. It wouldn't hurt at all."

Before she could respond, the lights flickered and then suddenly the house was plunged into darkness except for the light coming from the flames in the hearth.

"Whoa! Does this happen a lot?"

Justin put his fork down and told her, "Hang on for a minute." Justin went to the kitchen and returned with a flashlight. Let me go check the breaker box, and then…"

Justin paused and listened, walking to the front door and opening it before immediately shutting it. "The storm that was supposed to arrive tomorrow is here."

"What?!" Jessica went to the window and attempted to see outside. As her eyes adjusted, she saw the pine trees moving with the force of the wind. She could see snow blowing across the yard, and even more falling from the sky. "We haven't been home that long."

"Sometimes these storms come up suddenly. The combined weight of the snow and the wind becomes too much for the power lines to handle."

Jessica nodded. "How long will it be out for?"

Justin gave her a reassuring smile. "Probably until the storm abates. I can go start the generator if the dark bothers you."

Jessica shook her head. "No. I'm okay for right now."

"Good. Let's finish eating and then we can talk."

"I'm pretty much finished," Jessica told him, resuming her seat and pulling one of the afghans off the back of the couch to wrap around her shoulders.

"Are you cold?" he asked curiously.

"Not really. I just like having a blanket wrapped around me sometimes. So what did you want to talk about?"

"What brought you from Arizona?"

Jessica looked at him as he got up from the opposing couch and sat down next to her. "So? Why leave Arizona?"

"That's a really long story."

Justin looked at his wristwatch and told her, "We have plenty of time. I'll tell you what. I'll tell you something about myself, and then you can tell me something about you."

"Like twenty questions?" Jessica asked, intrigued by the man sitting in the glow of the fire. He was handsome in a rugged sort of way with wavy, dark brown hair and deep blue eyes that seemed to watch her carefully and see way too much.

"Sort of. I'll even start. I have two brothers, Mason and Kaillar."

Jessica giggled. "I already know that."

"Yes, but it's part of the complete package, so bear with me."

"Fine. Continue with your story." She waved at him.

"Well, I have no idea who my father is or was. I'm pretty sure my mother didn't know the answer to that either. My mother, in name only, was raised right here in Silver Springs, but had stars in her eyes. It seemed that her Christian upbringing was stifling her creative nature. As soon as she turned eighteen, she ran off to LA and then to Las Vegas. She wanted to see her name in bright lights and her face plastered across magazines and movie screens."

"That didn't happen?"

"Not quite. While waiting for her big break, she hooked up with the wrong people. They introduced her to drugs and alcohol. Mainly heroin. She managed to make it home each time one of us was born, but she never could make the rehab stick. The last time she left, after Kaillar was born, my Uncle Jed had to go to Las Vegas to pick up her corpse. They found her body beaten up and lying in an alley somewhere."

"How horrible!" Jessica said, covering her mouth as she tried to take in everything he was telling her. "Did they ever catch the people who did it?"

"As far as I know, they never even tried to find them. From what I've managed to piece together, the Las Vegas police considered her a junky and a lost cause."

"Wow! Just...wow!" Jessica sat there stunned. Their stories were so similar, and yet different. Telling him about her parents now seemed not so bad.

Justin looked at her and then nodded his head. "Your turn."

"How old were you when you came back to Silver Springs for good?"

"Eight. Uncle Jed had her buried next to her parents on the southern side of the mountain."

"I'm sorry, that must have been so hard on you and your brothers."

"It was." He looked up at her and then gave her a smile, wanting her to know that he'd shared something highly personal with her and lived to tell about it. "Your turn."

"How personal are we going to get here? I mean, this is your game."

Justin gave a self-deprecating laugh. "Normally my answer would be to steer clear of anything personal. But for some reason, I feel like I can talk to you. As if you might understand where others wouldn't."

"You've lost me there. I still don't understand."

"Let me ask you a question. You said you were raised by your grandmother and that your parents allowed themselves to get killed the first night we met."

"Did I?" she fired back, not sure she wanted to go down this memory lane filled with land mines.

"You did. Your exact words in fact. What did you mean by that? How did your parents allow themselves to get killed?"

Jessica sat there and shook her head. "I think it's still your turn. Tell me more about your mother."

"Fortunately, I was so young I don't remember much about her, and what I do remember isn't all that pleasant. There were times when I was growing up I wished I hadn't had any memories of her. That I could have looked at the pictures of when she was a child and listened to the stories Uncle Jed told and that would have been all I ever knew about her."

"But you have memories of her…"

"Memories of a drugged up, too skinny woman who was always promising to get herself together, and never could manage to leave the drugs and alcohol alone. I only spent a few weeks here and there with her, usually after she'd come home and dried out for a few weeks. She would then return to Las Vegas, the stars back in her eyes, and things would be good until she got tired of being turned down for some acting or modeling job."

Justin looked at her, shaking his head. "I'd rather not have had any memories of her than those. I know my uncle felt the same way. He used to say he had a hard time remembering her as a carefree young girl that would follow him and his friends around the mountains. I never saw that woman. Ever."

Chapter 16

She looked at him for a moment and tried to put herself in his position. *Would she have given up memories of her parents, even if they'd been bad?* All she'd ever wanted was a chance to know her parents, but hearing Justin's story made her somewhat glad that she didn't have any bad memories of them. No, she just didn't have any memories of them.

She looked down at her hands and then began, "My parents were missionaries to Africa. When my mother found out she was pregnant with me, they asked for furlough and came back to the states. Things would have been much different if they had stayed here."

"But they went back?" Justin filled in the rest of her story. When she nodded, he asked, "What happened?"

"Civil unrest led to the rise of a Salafist jihadist militant group with ties to the Middle East. They attacked the school where my parents conducted their work, killing all nine Americans."

"Including your parents," he added.

"Yeah."

"Were the men who murdered them ever brought to justice?"

Jessica nodded. "About three years ago. At least that's what the State Department reported. They should never have been there." She heard the anger in her voice and tried to push it down once again.

"I thought you said they were missionaries. Weren't they just going where God led them?"

Jessica huffed out a breath, her anger bright and fierce. "Yeah! Where God sent them! To die! I never have understood why he would send people who'd sacrificed everything to follow His teachings to their deaths."

She was shaking with emotion and when she dared look up, she couldn't stand the look in Justin's eyes. *Great!* "I suppose you believe in a loving God and want to offer me some empty platitudes about how my parents will have a greater reward in Heaven because they were martyrs. Well, I've heard it all my life and I don't buy it! He sent them over there to die, instead of letting them stay here and raise me. That doesn't sound like a loving God to me!"

When Justin started to speak, she shook her head and continued. "Shelley showed me some article the other day that talked about how much progress the church has made in South Africa. The writer commented that without the sacrifice of Christian missionaries like my parents, the current revival wouldn't have been possible."

"Was that a recent article?" Justin asked, turning to sit facing her on the couch.

"No. It was written several years after their deaths. But it doesn't matter."

"Of course it does. Your parents were martyred for Christ and the article was giving credit to their sacrifice."

Jessica looked up at him, tears in her eyes. "But why would God send them back over there just to die. He could have protected them. I know He could have. Growing up, I heard the stories of the miracles God performed for the children of Israel, and how blessed the disciples of the early Church were. If He could do all of those things, I know He could have spared my parents' lives!"

"So that you could have them back?" Justin asked softly.

"They were my parents!"

Justin reached for her hands, untangling her fingers and then clasping them lightly with her own. "Jessica, have you ever done wondered what drove your parents to leave their eighteen-month old baby behind? Did you ever think about how much they must have loved you to do that?"

"If they loved me they would have taken me with them." Jessica heard the words and then cringed. "But they were afraid for my safety, so they left me with my grandmother."

Justin was quiet as he let her mind sort things out. He thought maybe she was going in the right direction, and then she told him, "If God had truly cared about any of us, He would have kept them safe and prevented them from going back there!"

"But your parents had committed their lives to spreading the Good News to others. Have you ever been driven to do something? Something that others thought was stupid or crazy, but something inside of you told you to do anyway?"

Jessica shook her head "I don't think so. And I like to think that common sense would win any such conflict."

"What made you leave Arizona? You said you'd never left the state before. Why now?"

This was the part of the conversation she didn't want to have. Telling anyone about Jason's betrayal was akin to admitting how stupid she'd been. "I needed a change of scenery."

"Really? You decided to quit and move for no reason?"

Jessica looked up and realized this moment was a turning point for her. She'd not spoken about Jason to anyone. "I left Arizona because I was stupid. And tired of the past always being thrown in my face."

"I highly doubt that," he told her, holding onto her hands when she would have pulled them away.

Jessica gave a derisive laugh. "You won't say that in a few minutes."

"Try me," Justin challenged her.

"I went to college with a huge chip on my shoulder. I was finally out from under my grandmother's influence, and I was so tired of trying to live up to everyone's expectations of what I should be doing. I did all of the things I knew I shouldn't. And still, I never was truly happy. And then I met Thomas."

Justin watched the soft, sad smile form on her face and felt a stab of jealousy. *Thomas had really meant something to her.* He didn't want to ask, but a friend would do exactly that. So he did so, quietly. "Thomas broke your heart?"

Jessica cried and tears spilled over. "Yeah. He was such a cute kid. I met him during my first classroom clinical. He wasn't sick then, and he and I became cohorts in the classroom and on the playground. Then he got sick and missed a few weeks of school."

"What was wrong with him?" Justin asked, feeling guilty for having been jealous of a young boy.

"Cancer. A rare and aggressive form of cancer. He died a little while later. He had so much to live for, and yet God didn't protect him. He let that little boy die, destroying his parents and everyone who knew him."

"God didn't give him cancer. You know that right?" Justin asked her, the sight of her tears making his heart hurt.

"But He had it within His power to make it leave. Thomas hadn't done anything to deserve…"

"Whoa! Tell me you don't think bad things happen to people because they deserve it?"

Jessica didn't believe that and she hadn't meant to imply that she did. "No. I know that bad things happen to people sometimes, and I realize that people die, but why did God have to take Thomas?"

"I don't know," Justin told her, pulling her into his arms and rubbing his hand up and down her back. "I don't know, but we have to trust that God does know."

"I'm a little low in the trust department."

"Have you told Him how you feel?"

"Like He cares! I mean, my life couldn't have been worse, and then I met Jason. He swept down and made me smile again."

"Jason is?" Justin asked, not wanting to jump to conclusions again.

"My ex-boyfriend. I'm sure he doesn't even count me as that, but we were together for almost four years. The entire time he was playing me. He lived four hours away, and had gotten engaged to a very nice country club princess the week before he started college.

"At least he didn't officially ask me to marry him, just move in with him." *That would have been the ultimate humiliation!* "Luckily, I didn't do that. Something inside of me urged me to keep my own place."

"Where was your grandmother during all of this?" Justin asked, regretting the question as tears spilled out of her eyes.

Jessica took a shuddering breath and shook her head. "She died in March."

"Of this year?" Justin asked, feeling horrible if that were the case.

She nodded her head. "Yeah. I went back home and took care of her affairs, sold the house, paid off my student loans, and returned to school. I finished my Master of Education at the end of May and started working as a teacher's aide. I went by Jason's condo one day when we didn't have any students in the classroom. His fiancée had come for a visit."

Jessica stopped and pushed herself away from Justin, leaning back against the couch as she relived the humiliation she'd felt that day. "I feel so stupid," she murmured softly.

Justin was furious on her behalf. "What did you do?"

Jessica shook her head. "Nothing. I walked out, holed up in my apartment for the rest of the week and applied for about a dozen jobs out of state. When Paul Sherman called me three days later and interviewed me over the phone, I made up my mind that if he offered me the job I was going to take it. He called back an hour later, offered me the job, and I began making plans to leave Arizona."

"Didn't your ex try to explain himself?"

"I don't know. I quit answering his phone calls."

"The jerk didn't even try to talk to you?"

"That's for the best. I don't know what I would have told him."

Justin didn't believe that for a minute. "Oh, I think you could have found plenty of things to tell him. Why don't you try?"

"What?!" She looked up in shock.

"Pretend I'm the jerk and tell me what you would have told him. Let me have it. It's obvious to me that you haven't dealt with his betrayal yet, and since he's not anywhere close, pretend I'm him. Don't worry about offending me. I've got really thick skin. I can handle it."

"I couldn't do that…"

"You need to do this. I can hear the hurt and anger in your voice as if it just happened. It's been what, a few weeks?"

"Give or take a week."

"You need to heal, but before you can do that you need to get rid of some of the pain. Give it to me."

Chapter 17

Jessica could see that Justin was serious about her using him as a sounding board for her anger, pain and humiliation, but she wasn't sure letting go of her control was such a good thing.

"Jess, trust me on this. If I had a punching bag handy, I'd suggest you go beat on it for an hour or two, but I don't. I also am not going to offer myself up in that capacity. You may be little, but my guess is you can pack quite a punch in those little fists."

He tapped her fists and then kissed her knuckles before looking up at her again. "Trust me with your pain, Jess."

"I haven't told... I..." She lost control of her emotions and began to rail at him. She balled her fists up and pounded the couch. "How could he have treated me like that? How could I have been so stupid not to see what was happening? Three plus years I wasted on him. I shared my grief with him, and I thought he truly cared that I was hurting. I told him about my parents and he encouraged my anger, telling me that if God didn't care about me, why should I care about Him. I thought I had dealt with my grief, but then I found out all of it had been a lie."

She quit pounding the couch and looked at him, her breathing ragged as she sobbed. "I didn't deserve to be treated like that. I thought he cared." She collapsed against the back of the couch pressing her fists into her eyes.

Justin couldn't stand to watch her suffer and he pulled her fists away from her face, cradling her head against his chest. "Shush. Jess, I'm so sorry. He was an idiot and he's definitely not worth this much energy. You trusted the wrong person, and he let you down in a way that shouldn't have happened."

Her sobs continued, but he felt her body relax against his own and he settled back against the couch, keeping her close to him. He just sat there and let her cry. The fireplace crackled, the lights were still down, and as he sat there in the semi-dark trying to absorb her hurt, he realized that he wanted to be her rock. He wanted to help ease her hurts in the future, not just now.

He closed his eyes and his mind took a journey to a place in the future where the hurt had healed, and Jess was free to love and believe in herself and in others with joy in her heart. He wanted to be there when that happened. *But was she so damaged by the past and the hurt and anger she'd held onto that she wouldn't be able to let go of it? Only time would tell.*

When the fire began to die down and he felt the temperature of the house begin to drop, he shuffled her so that he could rise from the couch and add some more logs to the fire. She'd drifted off to sleep against his chest, and when he moved her away from him, she reached out for him and moaned in her sleep.

Well, she trusts me in her sleep. Now, if I can only get her to trust me when she's awake.

He glanced at his watch and realized it was almost 10:30 at night. He stepped into the kitchen and pulled out his cell phone. Mason answered on the second ring.

"Justin, you okay?"

"Yeah. I'm down here at Jessica's place. The power went out in town about an hour ago."

"We still have some power up here, but the way the wind is howling, I'm not sure how much longer that's going to last."

"Well, use the generator if you need to. I'm going to stay in town tonight. I don't want to risk driving the truck back up the mountain in this weather."

"Okay. Did Jeff leave the generator in place?"

"It's in the garage and there's fuel for it. I won't start it up unless I have to. We have enough wood to last until morning inside the house."

"Okay, what do you want me to tell Jeremy about the morning?"

Justin closed his eyes and groaned. "I forgot all about the morning." He'd offered to begin teaching the elementary Sunday School class several weeks ago, and tomorrow morning was his debut. "If you could bring me some clothes, I'd appreciate it. I'll be there."

"I can do that. See you in the morning."

Justin pocketed the phone and then returned to the living room. Jessica was still sleeping. He grabbed the extra blankets off the couches and made a sort of sleeping bag of sorts on the couch. When he went to lift her into the makeshift bed, she clutched at his shirt. "Don't leave me, please?"

"I'm not going anywhere. I just want you to be warm."

Jessica's eyes were puffy and her nose was stuffed up from her crying jag earlier. He could see she was having difficulty and asked, "What can I do to help?"

"Maybe a warm rag?" she murmured, trying to wipe her face off with the tissues that sat on the side table.

"Be right back." Justin returned moments later with a warm rag and a glass of water. "Here." He handed her both of them and then pulled a bottle of painkillers from his pocket. "I brought these along in case you need them."

Jessica looked at the bottle and shook her head. "No, I'm good."

He sat down next to her and felt the moment expand, and the tension between them grow. Unable to resist, he raised a hand and moved her hair behind her ear. "Feel any better?"

Jessica raised her eyes. "Maybe. I just feel raw. I haven't cried that much in a long time. Not even at my grandmother's funeral. Everyone was watching me, looking to see what I was going to do, and all I could think about was getting out of town again."

"Well, the grief doesn't go away all at once, but it slowly does get better. You just have to keep talking about your feelings. And I promise to be around to listen."

Jessica dropped her eyes and then he watched as she fidgeted, her fingers twisting themselves in the blankets. He covered her hand with his own and asked, "What's going through that head of yours?"

She shook her head and he tipped her chin up, forcing her to meet his eyes. He wished there was more light, but the intimacy of the moment wouldn't have been the same. "Tell me."

Trust me with your thoughts. That's what he was really asking her for and Jessica found for the first time in a long while, she really wanted to do just that. She lifted a hand and cupped his strong jaw. She'd not known this man for very long, so how was it she felt so connected to him. He'd gotten her to release some of the pent-up emotions surrounding her grandmother's death and her ex's betrayal – something she'd never done before.

She did feel better. Her anger was less potent, her grief not quite so sharp. And he hadn't run away!

Her thumb brushed the corner of his lips and she wondered what he would do if she leaned forward just a few inches...

She didn't have to wonder any longer. Justin lowered his head and placed his lips tenderly against her own. He didn't press or try to take the kiss beyond the simple sharing, and his heart reveled in the connection between them. Never before had a kiss felt so right!

He broke the kiss and watched her eyes. "That was nice."

"More than nice," she agreed, licking her bottom lip before biting it.

"Want to do it again?" Justin asked softly.

Jessica didn't need another invitation. She wrapped her arms around his neck and plastered her lips against his own. She was feeling so many things for this man, and kissing him seemed so natural. She could almost believe that Silver Springs was where she was meant to be.

Chapter 18

Two weeks later...

Justin was frustrated with Jessica's continued refusal to attend church with him. She'd made great progress in dealing with her grandmother's death and Jason's betrayal, but she still felt that God had betrayed her.

Thanksgiving was a week away, and this weekend was the church potluck and Thanksgiving celebration. Chloe had been working on her, as well as Shelley, and the other people in town she routinely saw throughout the week.

Their relationship seemed to be going well, but they were quickly approaching a crossroads where Justin would have to choose between her and his convictions. He couldn't, and wouldn't, abandon his church family or his faith in God. But he also couldn't imagine letting her go. To help the situation, he had arranged to have Sarah talk to Jessica.

He stopped by the school, flowers in hand, and saw her exit her classroom. "Hey!"

"Justin, what are you doing here?" She offered him an easy smile that seemed to light up her face and his world at once.

"I stopped by to escort you home. Here, these are for you."

Jessica accepted the flowers and then sniffed them. "Thank you. What's the occasion?"

"I was hoping you could help me with something this afternoon."

"Sure."

"Okay, let's drop your things off at the house and then you can ride with me."

"Where are we going?"

"Over to the small motel and boarding house. It's owned by a woman named Sarah. "

"What are we going to be doing there?"

"We're putting together the gifting baskets this afternoon. You don't mind helping, do you?"

Jessica shook her head. "No. I don't mind at all. Gifting baskets?"

Justin grabbed her hand as they stepped out into the cold afternoon. Daylight savings time had come and gone a week earlier, and it was already getting dark by the time most people got off of work. The sidewalks were cleared of snow, but there was another major storm coming later in the week, and Justin was hoping to speak with Jessica about spending the Thanksgiving holidays with him and his brothers, up at the lodge.

Scott and Chloe had been planning to come, but with their baby so close to being born, they didn't want to leave the safety of the town. And Doc Matthews. He had delivered most of the forty and under Silver Springs population, and Justin knew it was only a matter of time before a replacement would need to be found.

He waited in the living room while Jessica changed into a pair of jeans and a soft cable-knit sweater. She and Chloe had made a trip into Silverthorne a few days earlier, the school having closed to handle the elections taking place. It was the largest building in Silver Springs and it only made sense to use it as a polling place, but with their children's safety at risk, none of the parents seemed to mind an extra day off school to keep their children and the general population separated.

In truth, there were only a handful of people living in the county, that weren't known well by the community at large. But even one person could be a threat, and Justin applauded the school board for being so proactive in protecting the town's youngsters. He never wanted to see Silver Springs spread across the news media because someone had hurt their kids.

Jessica returned and he helped her up into his truck. After he seated himself and headed for the edge of town, she asked, "So, you seem to be deep in thought. What's up?"

Justin stared at her. "Am I that obvious?"

Jessica grinned at him. "To me."

He shook his head. "And here I was trying to figure out when would be the appropriate time to ask."

"Now seems like a really good time."

"Okay. But promise to hear me out before you say 'No'?"

"You seem to think you already know my answer."

Justin smiled at her. "Here goes. I want you to spend the Thanksgiving holiday with us up at the lodge."

"You want…but…" She cleared her throat. Silver Springs was a very tight-knit community and she was afraid that if people found out, they would think badly of her. "I don't think I can do that. People will talk."

Justin sighed. "I know. Chloe and Scott were supposed to be up there as well…"

"She can't leave town! The baby could come any day."

"I know," he nodded. "That's why they're not coming. But I don't want you to be alone, and I guess I'm being a little selfish. I want to spend those four days with you."

Jessica smiled at him. "I would like that as well, but..." She broke off as a crazy idea occurred to her. "How about...?" She looked at him and then nodded. "How about you and your brothers come down to town? There are plenty of unused bedrooms in the house. Scott and Chloe could use the other bedroom on the ground floor, and..."

Justin pulled his truck over and then grabbed her, pulling her close and kissing her. She giggled against his lips and finally managed to push him away so she could speak. "I take it that idea meets your approval?"

"Yes. Now come back here and kiss me."

Jessica gave in for another moment and then they both broke apart when a passing car honked at them. She sat back, touching her lips and watching him with a soft smile on her face. "You know this thing between us is kind of crazy, right?"

Justin shook his head. "No. I don't know anything of the kind. I've been waiting all of my life to meet someone I truly liked. That would be you."

"This is moving way too fast," she commented.

"We have as much time as we like. Now, let's go pack baskets."

Chapter 19

Packing the baskets had gone smoothly. Jessica had really liked Sarah, and she'd even offered to go back Friday and Saturday to help deliver the baskets. Justin and his brothers had been slated to help as well, but a multiple-car accident on the highway had taken them out of town all day Friday.

Saturday, a group of missing skiers had taken them out of town as well. Jessica had been disappointed, but also proud that Justin and his brothers were able to do so much good.

Sarah and she had just finished delivering the last basket, and were drinking coffee at Sarah's kitchen table, when the conversation turned personal again.

"So, Justin tells me you're not sure about church and God."

"What?" Jessica sputtered. "I don't know that I'm unsure about church. Or God. I know exactly who He is. I just don't think I need Him in my life."

Sarah looked at her for the longest time and then shook her head. "Denial only leads to heartache."

"Denial? I'm not in denial..."

"Sure you are. You grew up learning about God and His love, but when you tried to apply that to your own life and circumstances, you found Him lacking. You've been focusing on the wrong things."

Jessica was hurt and angry that the friendship she'd had with this woman was going to end badly. "I don't want to talk about this."

"Good. Then listen. I've been where you are. I married my high school sweetheart, Brad Jenkins. We were so very happy, and we started this little motel and boarding house together. Things were going so well, but Brad felt strongly that he needed to join the service.

"I wasn't exactly on board with the idea, but he had it all planned out. He would join the service and then once his time was up, he'd go to college using his GI status, and we could take the motel to the next level. He wouldn't have to pay for college, and he'd have a steady income to send back home while he was active."

"So what happened?"

"He made it through basic training, and then joined a special training program. It was all very hush-hush, and he never could tell me exactly what he was being trained for. But it was also very dangerous. I found that out firsthand when two uniformed officers came knocking on the door his fifth month into their program. They regretted to inform me that there had been a training accident and Brad had been killed in the line of duty."

"Oh no! Did they ever tell you what happened?"

"No! I didn't even get his remains back. I never really got a good answer regarding that, but it didn't matter. We had a closed-casket service, and I had to deal with the knowledge that my husband was gone forever. I was so mad at God for taking him from me. Brad had been following his conscience, and we both felt at peace with the knowledge that God wanted him to do this."

"How could you be at peace after what happened?" Jessica asked, wondering how this woman got past the hurt and anger. She'd seen firsthand over the last few days how this woman felt about God. She lived her life to do His will, but why?

"Look, Jessica. God never promised any of us a walk in the park. Life is hard, and bad, horrible things happen to people who don't deserve it. Good people die. Bad people live. But we have to focus beyond all that."

"How? How do you look the other way when God allows bad things to happen?" Jessica was thinking about Thomas and how crushed his parents had been at his funeral. And yet... They'd not railed at God. She hadn't really taken time to analyze it at the time, but they'd rejoiced in the knowledge that their little boy wasn't suffering anymore and was in the arms of Jesus.

"Jess, let me ask you a question. You told me about the little boy with cancer and honestly, I think losing a child would hurt much worse than losing Brad ever did. But I haven't ever gone down that road, so I can only guess. But if you could have chosen for Thomas to live another ten years, knowing that he would be in horrible pain, and undergo medical procedure upon procedure, would you have chosen that instead of letting him die quickly and without years of torture?"

"Of course I would have. But see, you're assuming he would have been sick anyway. Why did God allow him to get sick in the first place? I've read my Bible and I've heard all the stories of great healings, both in days gone by and in other places around the world, so why not Thomas?"

"Do you believe Thomas is in Heaven? Do you believe your parents are there as well?"

"Yes. But that doesn't..."

"Think about it before you start trying to go down that road. If they are in Heaven, we will see them again. God simply took them home first. Who knows what tragedies might have awaited them here on earth if they had stayed. And yes, it is hard on those left behind. But we don't have to go through it alone."

"I've always felt alone. Even when I found Jason, my ex, and I thought he understood, he didn't. I was just an easy girlfriend at college because his fiancée was four hours away. I shared things with him, thinking he truly was sympathetic, but in reality, he was just going through the motions to humor me and keep me complacent."

"He sounds like a real piece of work and you're much better off without him."

"I know that. Until Justin..."

"Yes?" Sarah asked with a twinkle in her eyes.

"Well, I really like him and he says the same, but he doesn't understand why I can't trust God."

"Neither do I. Have you ever stopped to think about all of the blessings He's bestowed upon you?"

"Blessings? What blessings?"

"That answers my question. Thursday is Thanksgiving. Why don't you take some time over the next few days and try to answer that question. I promise you if you will, you'll start thinking about things a whole lot differently."

Jessica didn't think so, but after several more minutes, she promised to think on the issue. She even promised to share some of those blessings, provided she could come up with some, with Justin the next time she saw him.

Chapter 20

Jessica spent Saturday night alone. Justin and his brothers had found the lost hikers, but one of them needed medical attention, and all three brothers had ended up in Vail at the hospital. They decided to spend the night, but Justin had promised to come back at first light, saying his Sunday School class was counting on him.

He'd once again urged Jessica to come to church with him, but she once again refused. Not as vehemently as she had in weeks past, but she refused nonetheless. After hanging up the phone, she heated up a bowl of soup and sat in front of the fire, her mind replaying everything Sarah had told her.

Blessings? What counted as a blessing?

Her mind drifted back to her childhood when the ladies in the church were always telling her how lucky she was to have her grandmother. *Okay, that could be a blessing. Number one. Yay!*

Her grandmother had been a blessing. If she hadn't been around and willing to raise a young child, even though she was advanced in her years, Jessica might have ended up in South Africa with her parents. She could have been killed, or worse yet, taken as a hostage.

Okay, her grandmother really was a blessing.

As she thought about her life, she started adding more blessings to the list. *Grandma always had plenty of food and money to buy the things they truly needed. No, Jessica didn't get everything she'd wanted, but she had everything she needed and a little more.*

She'd been raised in a Christian household, giving her life to Jesus when she was only six. She'd known she was loved.

She'd gotten into the college of her choice. Her grades had been good enough to earn her a partial scholarship. She'd thumbed her nose at God, but still she'd never felt abandoned by Him.

That thought caused her to pause. *She'd abandoned God, but in her spirit, she'd always known He was waiting in the wings. Wow!*

That thought floored her. She'd done everything wrong and still, somehow, God had been there waiting for her to come back around. She jumped forward to Jason. That hadn't been God, that had been all her. She'd ignored the small voice inside her head, warning her he wasn't the right one. She'd set herself up for failure.

She tried to stay mad at God for taking her grandmother, but the woman was 92 when she passed away, and she'd done so in her sleep. She hadn't suffered, or had to suffer the indignities of being moved into a nursing home. She'd died peacefully in her sleep with her Bible clutched to her chest.

Tears filled her eyes as she realized how unfair she'd been to God. She'd held onto her anger, hoping to use it as a shield against the pain of loss, but had only succeeded in hurting herself in the process.

She fell to the floor, tears streaming down her face as she cried out to God to forgive her unbelief and misplaced anger. She used the entire box of tissues, and still the tears flowed.

Tears for her parents. Tears for her grandmother. Tears for the little boy and his family that would never see him grow up. She even shed some tears over Jason. For the emptiness that had to exist inside the man – otherwise, he wouldn't have been able to treat her so callously.

On a whim, she took a page from Justin's catharsis book and fired up her laptop. She pulled up Jason's email address and typed him a quick note.

Jason,

I know you will be shocked to read this, but I needed to send this for my own healing. I feel sorry for you and for your future wife. You used me for your own purposes, callously abusing my emotions, my time, and my energy, all so that you wouldn't have to face being alone while at college.

I'm here to tell you that I forgive you for doing it. I've discovered something that I hope one day you'll experience as well. Even though I turned my back on God, he never turned His back on me. I've started to make things right with Him, and part of that involved forgiving you.

So, I forgive you. I also pray that before you and your fiancée get married, you will do some soul searching and see if you aren't running from God as well.

Please don't contact me as I am putting that part of my life behind me. I'm taking the lessons I've learned with me, and I hope you do the same. I wish you a happy life. Please know that I am doing everything in my power to find a happy life for myself.

Jess

She hit send, and then closed the computer. She felt better! Amazingly, she truly did feel as if that part of her life was over. But there was still something missing. She didn't have anyone to share her transformation with.

She thought about calling Chloe, but didn't want to upset the mother-to-be. She thought about calling Sarah, but it was almost midnight, and she figured the woman would already be in bed. She turned down the lights, and then she remembered how her grandmother had always celebrated, after Jessica had gone to bed.

Her grandmother would turn on some worship music, and spend time with God. Singing. Praying. Talking. It didn't matter, but she'd spied on her grandmother more than once and been amazed at how happy she'd seemed during those moments.

She retrieved her computer and found an online Christian radio station. She turned the audio player on and just listened. Song after song talked about God as a friend, as a shelter in the midst of the storm, as a good father. She sat there in the dark and let the words soak into her spirit.

She drifted off to sleep at some point, her computer battery finally dying as well, plunging the house into peace and quiet.

She woke up as the sun peeked through the windows and sat up on the mattress. She hadn't even changed her clothes the night before, but she still felt refreshed!

She glanced at the clock and suddenly felt a sense of urgency. Church was due to start in twenty minutes, and she'd never before felt such a strong desire to be there. She didn't have any skirts, but she donned a pair of corduroys, a sweater, and her boots. The church was located three blocks away, so she grabbed her keys and was pulling into the parking lot as the church bells rang out announcing the morning service was about to begin.

She felt very uncomfortable as she got out of her car, and really wished she didn't have to walk into the church by herself. A pair of arms wrapped around her neck.

"Jessica! Welcome!"

Jessica looked up into the eyes of Shelley, and standing right behind her was Sarah. She gave the woman a hug and then walked to Sarah. "Thank you. I did what you suggested, and…" She broke off as tears filled her eyes.

"Enough of that. This is a morning of celebration. Come on. Justin's going to be so thrilled!"

The two women bracketed her, each taking an elbow and escorting her into the small church building. She saw Mason and Kaillar sitting towards the back, and gave them a small smile when they grinned at her, and Kaillar gave her a thumbs up.

Justin was down front, talking to Pastor Jeremy, but the whispers of her arrival quickly reached his ears. He looked up, and the smile that split his face was one she would never forget. It was filled with joy and...love? He came towards her, almost running down the aisle.

"Jessica! You're here!"

"I'm here. I have so much to tell you, but..."

"Later. Come, let's sit down. I want to hear about everything, but right now, I want to enjoy having you sitting beside me during the service."

Jessica allowed him to escort her back to the pew he shared with his brothers. She did her best to brush off her rusty hymn-singing skills, finally remaining silent and just allowing the moment to wash over her.

She'd come to Colorado to escape the events and her past in Arizona. She'd not only found a new beginning in her career and her love life, she'd found a new beginning with the One who had made all things possible.

As the service continued, she couldn't wait for the coming weeks and months ahead. She was where God wanted her to be, and she was determined to live every moment and make it count.

Thank You

Dear Reader,

Thank you for choosing to read my books out of the thousands that merit reading. I recognize that reading takes time and quietness, so I am grateful that you have designed your lives to allow for this enriching endeavor, whatever the book's title and subject.

Now more than ever before, Amazon reviews and Social Media play vital role in helping individuals make their reading choices. If any of my books have moved you, inspired you, or educated you, please share your reactions with others by posting an Amazon review as well as via email, Facebook, Twitter, Goodreads, -- or even old-fashioned face-to-face conversation! And when you receive my announcement of my new book, please pass it along. Thank you.

For updates about New Releases, as well as exclusive promotions, visit my website and sign up for the VIP mailing list. Click here to get started: www.morrisfenrisbooks.com

I invite you to connect with me through Social media:
1. Facebook   :
   https://www.facebook.com/AuthorMorrisFenris/
2. Twitter: https://twitter.com/morris_fenris
3. Pinterest: https://www.pinterest.com/AuthorMorris/
4. Instagram:
   https://www.instagram.com/authormorrisfenris/

For my portfolio of books on Amazon, please visit my Author Page:

Amazon USA:
amazon.com/author/morrisfenris

Amazon UK:
https://www.amazon.co.uk/Morris%20Fenris/e/B00FXLWKRC

You can also contact me by email:
authormorrisfenris@gmail.com

With profound gratitude, and with hope for your continued reading pleasure,

Morris Fenris
Author & Publisher

10493686R00067

Printed in Great Britain
by Amazon